THE ARCHDRUID OF MACCLESFIELD
Book Four of the Runford Chronicles

by
Rex Merchant

Published by
Rex Merchant @ Norman Cottage
89 West Road
OAKHAM
Rutland LE15 6LT UK

British Library Cataloguing-in-Publication Data.
A catalogue record of this book is available from the British Library

Cover graphics by Roy Pack. Typeset, printed and bound by Rex Merchant @ Norman Cottage.

THE ARCHDRUID OF MACCLESFIELD

Book Four of the Runford Chronicles

by

Rex Merchant

Published by
Rex Merchant @ Norman Cottage

Introduction

The fictitious town of Runford is in the flat, South Lincolnshire, fen country. The inhabitants of these fens are sturdy, independent folk, like their Viking ancestors before them.

They can appear uncommunicative and are often reserved with strangers, but their reticence should not be mistaken for a lack of intelligence or for slowness of thought. Like the rivers that drain this area, a still surface can hide deep waters and a busy undercurrent.

The Runford Chronicles are fictional but if such fantasies were to happen, the Lincolnshire fens would be one of the most likely places for them to occur.

Who's to say they have not already happened?

Rex Merchant
Oakham

Chapter One

The heavy stool crashed onto the bar floor. Howls of laughter filled the Duck and Dumplings public house. Paddy, the barman, glanced up from the racing pages in his evening paper, disturbed by the noise and curious to know what had caused so much amusement.

"I tell you, Albert Williams has finally lost his marbles. He was just coming out of his woods as I drove past on my way here. He was wearing his dressing gown, in broad daylight, on the main road."

"You mean he had a dressing gown over his other clothes?"

"No! He had a white dressing gown on and his bare legs were sticking out below the hem like a pair of pipe cleaners. He'd obviously got damn all else underneath it!"

As the regulars laughed even louder, the barman chuckled at the unlikely joke and returned to his reading. Albert was inclined to go overboard when he took up a new hobby, but he was an intelligent old fellow. What they were saying sounded very unlikely. He had just returned his attention to the racing pages when the street door swung open. Paddy glanced up to greet the newcomer, saw it was Albert Williams and took a curious second look at the way he was dressed. The barman allowed his eyes to travel over the coat the old chap was wearing, and down to Albert's bare legs, which protruded from a white towelling hem below his coat. The newspaper slipped through Paddy's fingers. For once the worldly barman was dumbstruck.

The regulars at the Duck and Dumplings were not struck so dumb. They voiced their opinions loudly.

"Is that a dress under that coat, Albert? Did you buy it from Oxfam or is it one of Dior's creations?"

"Take your coat off and have the next waltz with me."

"Well I'll be damned! Albert Williams, what are you doing wearing a nightdress hidden under your top coat? What are you supposed to be man, a closet transvestite?"

Albert frowned and glanced down at his legs. His face was a picture of confusion when he realised he'd failed to put on his trousers. From his pained expression, it was obvious that trousers had completely slipped his mind. He had forgotten how vague he could be when he was immersed in a new interest. The old chap recovered his wits quickly and decided to brazen it out. He drew himself up to his full five feet two inches, glared challengingly around the bar and answered his tormentors.

"It's not a nightdress, it's a towelling bathrobe, I mean, it's a toga. And I am not a transvestite. I'm a Druid!" He struck an imposing pose, one hand over his heart and the other held out in front of him like a Shakespearean actor in full flow.

"I am Pollawsdoc, the first of the modern fenland Druids. And I have the official licence and the psychic powers to prove it."

Momentarily the regulars were silenced by Albert's speech, for they could see he was serious. The veins stood out on his neck. His scalp blushed red, clearly visible through the thin covering of long grey hairs he brushed over his bald patch.

Albert finished his speech and crossed his arms aggressively over his chest. Unfortunately that action raised the hem of his coat even higher, revealing his knobbly knees and several more inches of bare, skinny legs, covered in a thatch of dark hairs and ending in a pair of muddy running shoes.

The sight was too much for them. Once again the drinkers at the bar dissolved into helpless laughter, slapping each other's backs and lodging their pint glasses on the bar top for safety. Even when Albert ignored them and turned his back on them to order a pint of Fenland Brew for himself, the raucous chorus of guffaws continued unabated.

Tony Tompkins was in the far corner of the bar having a quiet drink with a young female colleague. The girl had her back to the door, but Tony could see all that was happening. The young teacher slithered

3

down in his chair and slumped forward, deliberately letting his lank hair fall over his face as he tried to hide himself behind a narrow pillar.

"Oh my God! It's Uncle Albert," he muttered softly under his breath, but that involuntary comment was not spoken low enough to escape his pretty companion's hearing.

"Where?" She turned to look in the direction of the crowd at the bar, then smiled enquiringly at Tony. "If he's your Uncle Albert, I really would like to meet him."

Tony shrugged his shoulders sheepishly, trying to deny his involvement, but he knew he had made a big mistake bringing Diana Scullery to the Duck and Dumplings that evening. He smiled wanly, and made some lame excuses.

"He's busy with his cronies… He's probably just dropped in for a quick one on his way home from swimming… Perhaps I'll ask him over when he's free... Maybe you could meet him some other evening"

Tony was well aware everyone had days when things were destined to go wrong. Those days when life's lubrication came laced with a filling of coarse grit. On such occasions it was better to stay in bed. He knew he was really having one of those disasters when he saw his uncle look over in his direction.

Albert spotted his nephew and strode across the bar towards the young couple, the hem of his white dressing gown clearly showing below his coat.

"Tony boy, is that you beneath all that hair? I'm glad I've seen you. I've had such a moving experience, I just had to call in here to celebrate on my way home...In fact I was so elated I seem to have forgotten to...er... put on my trousers." The old man was obviously very excited about something. Placing his beer on the table between his nephew and the girl, he pulled up a chair, sat down and beamed at them both.

Diana's blue eyes grew large and saucer-like as she took in the full impact of Albert's appearance. Tony groaned and shook his head when he realised there was no escaping his embarrassing relative. Brushing back his curtain of dark hair, he forced a brave smile and introduced them

"Diana Scullery, the newly appointed Biology teacher at Runford Upper School." Tony waved a limp hand at his attractive blonde drinking partner, then turned to face the strange figure in the coat and dressing gown. "This is my Uncle Albert ... Albert Williams, my mother's older brother. He's a bit of a ...he's a bit of an old... an old ... eccentric." The last word came to him only after a long search and the rejection of several less polite alternatives. Tony knew from bitter experience that Albert was always up to something strange. That was part and parcel of his personality. In some ways Tony was proud of his uncle's independent way of thinking. As a boy, left fatherless when he was still very young, Tony had always looked up to Albert as a father figure, but occasionally the old man's antics crossed the line of normal acceptable behaviour. The locals at the Duck and Dumplings knew his uncle of old and indulged him, apart from some harmless leg pulling. His family had long since ceased to worry about the old chap. But Diana Scullery was new to the area and to Uncle Albert's weird ways. Tony was livid at this chance meeting because he fancied the girl and was trying to impress her favourably.

Albert frowned. "Scullery? That's a most unusual name. It sounds as if..."

Tony interrupted him. "Not half as unusual as you calling at the pub in a dressing gown." He hissed the words in his uncle's ear, anxious to stop him insulting his companion.

Diana ignored the reference to her surname "Did I hear you say, you're a Druid?" She asked the question innocently and sweetly, her distinctive blue eyes growing even wider as she looked the old man up and down.

"Not just 'A Druid,' my girl. I'm the first fenland Druid of modern times. I'm the local High Priest of the Holy Oak and a disciple of the Mysterious Mistletoe." Albert wiped his fingers on the hem of his towelling gown and extended a grubby, blood-stained hand in greeting.

"Sounds very impressive, Uncle. But who says you're all those dignitaries?" Tony had still not forgiven the old man for spoiling his date with Diana. In a tone loaded with sarcasm, he continued. "I suppose you'll be telling us there's an Archdruid at

Canterbury who confers all these high sounding honours?"

"No. He's not in Canterbury, lad. He's in Macclesfield!"

Tony thumped his forehead with his fist in disbelief.

Albert delved into his toga pocket and pulled out a roll of parchment patterned paper, with a thick wax seal dangling on a red ribbon attached to the bottom of it. He spread the impressive looking document on the table and put on his reading glasses.

"This is my official licence to practise druidism."

Tony picked up the certificate and glanced at the cheap paper and the commercial Gothic print.

"How much did this Archdruid fellow charge you for this?"

"Never you mind, lad. But I can tell you it was worth every penny. As you know, I have been studying world religions for years. Not one of them has produced such startling results as this druidism. Not even the Yoga Meditationers…they promised I would learn to fly … trouble was … they couldn't say exactly when."

"And I suppose you're going to tell us you've levitated after only one druid lesson?"

"Well, no… not exactly."

"Look, Uncle Albert. I don't mean to pour cold water on your hopes, but this new name you've been given. Pollawsdoc isn't it?" Tony ran his finger along the lines of printed Gothic script until he located the hand-written name. "Has it ever occurred to you to reverse the spelling?"

Albert squinted at the parchment and shook his head.

Diana read the name and raised her hand to her mouth to stifle a giggle.

"Pollawsdoc is only Codswallop spelled backwards. Shouldn't that tell you something about this druidism? It sounds a proper load of old Codswallop to me!"

Albert gave his nephew a long cold stare. It was obvious the lad hadn't a clue about religious matters. Tony might be a qualified teacher and have a degree in Medieval History but that didn't make him an expert on world religions. Albert raised a grubby finger as if he was lecturing a wayward child. Slowly and painstakingly, he explained.

"The ability to take jibes and not get ruffled is one of my celestial goals. It's written in my licence. It's like turning the other cheek." He wagged his finger at his nephew, in time to the words, to drive the message home. "Can you think of a better way to practice the art of humility than to poke fun at your own name? Look what happened just now when I came in the door. I gave those silly oafs something to talk about and I couldn't care less what they think of me. The knack is to keep your dignity."

"You're telling me you knew all along about this pun on your name? You don't mind being made fun of and paying for the privilege? Wait 'til I tell mum about this."

"You needn't do any such thing. Don't tell your mother anything. This is my business not my sister's. Promise me, Tony; not one word to Freda. Please." The reaction of his drinking friends to his new interest, was one thing, but Freda's sharp tongue was entirely another.

"Alright, I'll not tell mother, but tell me honestly, on your druid's honour, did you know about this ridiculous name?"

"Well, not exactly. I should have realised though. It's just another one of the hidden esoteric mysteries, the lessons keep mentioning."

Tony shrugged his shoulders. He knew it was useless protesting when the old fellow was addicted to one of his enthusiasms. Whenever Albert took up a new craze, it always burned white hot in the early days. Buddhism had lasted six months. Even Freda Tompkins, Tony's mother, had become used to seeing her brother sitting cross-legged in the market place, his begging bowl at his bare feet, a brass bell in his hand and his saffron robe billowing about him in the breeze. On market days, schoolchildren filled his bowl with their leftover, cold chips. Visitors came from miles away, just to see him and be photographed beside him. The South Holland Tourist Board had offered to list him as a being of special cultural interest. Even the market had doubled in size.

Diana wiped a tear of suppressed laughter from her cheek and grinned at Tony. "I think I will enjoy teaching at Runford Upper School. This fenland area has a lot to offer in the way of unusual entertainment."

Tony's sarcastic jibes were wasted on Albert. He was immersed in a rose coloured, incense scented, world of his own. When he had made the official druid sacrifice at his altar in Beggars Bush Wood, he knew something wonderful and supernatural had happened. There was no getting away from it. The ceremony had succeeded beyond his wildest expectations. A gentle breeze had sprung up in answer to his prayers, carrying the subtle scents of moist woodland and crushed grass. It rustled in the leaves of the oak trees above his head. Then the crowning achievement happened. A mythical beast had materialised from nowhere, and crept up to the altar, devouring the sacrificial offering before his very eyes. When he pictured the creature's sleek animal body and powerful birdlike head and wings, he felt a tingle travel down his spine, like an electric shock running from the rolled collar of his gown to the draughty split up the back. Wasn't that single manifestation proof enough of the truth of his new religion? This Druidism business promised untold possibilities. Metaphysically speaking, his horizons had expanded beyond anything he had ever imagined.

Albert had only one regret. He had not thought to take a camera to catch proof- positive of the beast on film. He knew the scoffing world of non-believers would only accept tangible evidence of his success. It was the same problem that dogged the UFO watchers; they never seemed to have a loaded camera handy when the aliens showed up. Tomorrow he would borrow an instant Polaroid camera, get some plastic Mistletoe, buy another sacrificial animal from the butcher, and repeat the entire ceremony.

Chapter Two

It was mid afternoon at Runford Upper School. Barry Dickinson, a sixth former studying history under Tony Tompkins, stealthily led the way from the side entrance of the school towards the bicycle sheds. He signalled his younger companion to duck below the level of the classroom windows so they would pass undetected.

"Keep your bloody head down, Sparky, otherwise the woodwork master will see you."

Ian Sparks dropped onto all fours and crawled along the ground after his friend. Once they were safely behind the bicycle sheds, Dickinson straightened up and led his friend to the far end, where there was a narrow alleyway separating the wooden end of the bike shed from the red brick boundary wall of the school field.

"Right. Give us a fag."

Sparky produced two thin rollups from his jacket pocket and a small cigarette lighter. The two boys relaxed with their backs pressed against the overlapping wooden boards and dragged contentedly on their illicit smokes.

"How come... you got... out of PE?" Sparky coughed.

"Told Muldoon I had a bad leg."

"Did he buy it? "

"Not at first, but I'd put a pebble in my shoe and it hurt like hell, so I limped rather convincingly. Anyway he seemed in too much of a hurry to get the lads running around the perimeter of the field to bother with me. Once they had left the gym, he vanished. "

"Gone for a crafty fag himself, I bet."

"Not him! He's a keep fit fanatic. Reckons he was a drill sergeant in the marines. Pity he ever left them and came here. I don't know why old 'fitness' Ford had to leave last term. He'd hardly reached retiring age. Anyway we're stuck with Captain-bloody-Marvel Muldoon, whether we like it or not! What about you? How did you get out of woodwork?"

"Easy. I told the teacher I had been ordered to see the headmaster's secretary."

The two boys lapsed into silence and enjoyed the brief pleasure of Sparky's weedy roll ups. The matchstick thin cigarettes, which Ian fashioned from his mother's discarded dog ends, burned brightly as the schoolboys sucked hungrily on them. The red glow raced nearer to their puckered lips at each successive drag.

"Reckon we'll get wet?" Dickinson looked up, turning his eyes to watch the sky above the passageway as the narrow band of blue change to threatening grey. He blew his cigarette smoke towards the clouds, trying unsuccessfully to look cool and produce smoke rings.

"We can always slip inside the bike shed if…" Sparky stopped in mid sentence. "…What's that noise? Hell! Somebody's coming this way!"

The boys hastily stamped out their dog ends and frantically fanned their hands to disperse the telltale signs of cigarette smoke. Footsteps could be heard coming towards them along the pathway they had just used.

"Quick! Up on the roof!" Dickinson whispered in Sparky's ear. The two boys braced their backs against the brick wall and their feet on the slatted wood of the bicycle shed and clambered up onto the sloping roof. Just in time they pulled their bodies onto the top of the bicycle shed as someone rounded the corner and halted in the alleyway they had just vacated.

The boys lay on their backs, hardly daring to breathe. Above them the threatening clouds scudded overhead. Below them they could hear the new arrival's rapid breathing. Suddenly, in a flurry of fast running steps, a second person burst onto the scene.

"Ah there you are, ma'am. Good." A deep male voice broke the silence.

"It's Muldoon!" Dickinson mouthed silently, his eyes wide with fear. If he got caught, how was he going to explain his ability to climb onto the bike-shed roof with an injured foot?

Sparky glared at him and held a warning finger up to his lips.

Below them, the answering voice was light and unmistakably feminine. "I can't stay long. Did anyone see you coming?"

The boys frowned at each other in disbelief.

"No. I sent my class on ten circuits of the rugby field. That will keep them busy for the whole lesson…You?"

"Free period. I'm supposed to be preparing for my next biology class."

Dickinson looked stunned. He clutched Sparky by the arm and pointed dramatically in the direction of the speakers. Sparky hutched himself closer to his friend, raising his eyebrows in question. "It's Miss Scullery, the new biology teacher! And she's meeting Muldoon behind the bike sheds!" Dickinson mouthed directly into his friend's ear. Below them the teachers' voices dropped to a low, conspiratorial whisper. The boys strained to hear what was being said.

"…I jog past the place every day but I can't see how we could get in …" Muldoon said.

"Only yesterday evening I found out Tony Tompkins might have a useful contact…I am working on him." Diana Scullery confided.

The voices went even lower. No matter how much he strained his ears Dickinson, who was nearest to the edge of the roof, could make out nothing more of their conversation. Suddenly, Muldoon swore and the clandestine meeting broke up.

"Damn it, ma'am! Must go. My class will be finishing their run."

The boys heard the PE master sprint away from the alleyway towards the gymnasium. Miss Scullery waited until Muldoon was well away, then walked hurriedly back towards the science block. Dickinson rolled over on his stomach and raised his head just above the ridge of the shed roof, to watch the retreating figure.

"She's a bit of alright, that Miss Scullery. But I don't like her choice of boyfriend." He watched the young blonde woman in the white lab coat until she vanished into the school building.

"Phew! That was too bloody close! " Sparky breathed a sigh of relief. "What was it they said about Mr Tompkins?" Suddenly a novel thought hit him. His face lit up. "I say! Do you suppose they came out here for a snog?"

"I didn't hear any bloody snogging! Did you?"

`"Well no…but why else would they meet in secret?"

"Search me? Anyway I'm damn pleased Muldoon didn't catch me. He's an evil bastard when he's crossed. He had the lower sixth doing press-ups for an entire lesson, last week, just because they were a few minutes late getting changed."

The boys climbed down from their hiding place and crept back into the school.

Dickinson said. "I shall never look at Muldoon the same way again. The lucky bastard! Fancy having it off with Miss Scullery."

"I thought you said nothing happened?" Sparky grabbed his mate by the lapels.

"No, nothing happened out there. But it stands to reason it has...or it soon will, otherwise why meet in secret and why all that whispering?"

"Rubbish! They were probably planning a surprise for Mr Tompkins. You're in his history group. Is it his birthday or something?"

"How should I know, or care, if it's a teacher's ruddy birthday?" Dickinson thumped Sparks in disgust.

Sparks stepped back out of reach and taunted. "Trust you to think they are having it off. You think of nothing but sex! My older sister says you are at that difficult age and have an overactive imagination." He pushed his friend against the wall and ran off down the deserted corridor to rejoin his woodwork class.

Dickinson was stung by the reference to Sparky's sister, a girl he had fancied for ages. He was about to give chase when he remembered his fake injury and the fact that the PE lesson was almost at an end. He turned and hobbled slowly towards the gymnasium.

Chapter Three

Tony Tompkins sprinted from the school playing field and was first out of the showers. He had been refereeing a second eleven match that Saturday morning and was rushing to meet Diana Scullery to take her out to lunch. Tony had chatted up the new teacher in the staff room. To his delight, he had found her surprisingly friendly. When he picked her up from the Biology lab he was still dragging a comb through his long wet hair.

"I hope I haven't kept you waiting. I was as quick as I could be in the locker room. I would have been quicker but Muldoon hadn't unlocked the showers. He's new so I'll have to forgive him, but he ought to be quicker off the mark than that."

"Who? Muldoon? Oh! You mean the PE teacher who started here this term, the same as me. I've not met him yet to speak to. Anyway, you haven't kept me waiting, Tony. I needed some time on my own to sort out the prep room cupboards." She waved her hand vaguely in the direction of the laboratory, stepped into the corridor and locked the door behind her. "There's a lot of outdated equipment in the biology department. That was dusty work. Let's go and get a drink, and something to eat."

"Fish and chips and coke suit you? " He drove them into town in his battered Sierra.

At the café, they managed to get seated in the front window. The locals considered this the best table as people passing by on the pavement could see what was happening; consequently portions were bigger and the service was much quicker. They chatted together as they ate.

"It was nice of you to invite me out again, Tony." Diana thanked him between mouthfuls of haddock, chips and mushy peas. "I hate the first few weeks at a new school. No one knows you and they all keep a polite distance."

Tony smiled broadly. When she had suggested they go out for a meal together, he had jumped at the chance of getting to know his new colleague, for she was a stunning looking girl.

"Don't give it another thought," he reassured her. "I'm local. A Lincolnshire Yellowbelly, born and bred here in the fens. In fact, I'm almost a Slodger and..."

"Slodger? What's one of those?"

"Ah! That's an old local word for the fen men who shot and trapped wildfowl for a living... Anyway, as I was saying, I'll enjoy showing you everything." In fact, I'll show you mine if you'll show me yours, he thought hopefully.

Tony sipped his coke and admired the girl out of the corner of his eye. With her long blonde hair, blue eyes and dimples, she was his idea of an ideal woman. He let his gaze slip down from her face, following the contours of her tight sweater. The pub sign at the Duck and Dumplings flashed into his mind. Then, prompted by the café's gaudy décor of painted coconut palms on tropical beaches, he imagined her topless, swaying to the music of a Hawaian guitar. In his vision, her bare breasts jiggled rhythmically to the island beat. She was dressed only in a sparse grass skirt. His thoughts turned to the garden shears he used to trim the long grass on his mother's lawn. The stupid grin on his face almost gave him away.

"What's the matter? Have I spilled some ketchup?" She self-consciously wiped her handkerchief over her lips, then glanced down at her jumper, completely misreading his attentions.

"No...NO! I was thinking of something that happened in class yesterday afternoon," he lied lamely. "It was just before the bell. We were discussing the South Sea Boobs...Sorry. No! ...NO!...The South Sea Bubble..." He coughed to hide his embarrassment, pretending to choke on his fizzy drink. She leaned over and patted his back, forgetting their conversation and conveniently letting him off the hook.

Over lunch they discussed what they would do with the rest of the day.

"I'm free now. My car and I are at your disposal, Diana."

"Do call me Di. All my friends do. I will take you up on your kind offer. I need to call on the Steinn Brothers research plant down Beggars Bush Lane, and arrange a school visit to their laboratories."

Tony knew all about Steinn Brothers. They owned a large site just outside the town. The laboratories occupied land previously farmed by his Uncle Albert. The Steinn Brothers industrial site covered fifty acres of prime fen farmland, off Beggars Bush Lane. It was built alongside a ten-acre wood, which Albert had kept for his own use, retaining the wooded area as a nature reserve. The old man had spent years managing the woodland and couldn't bear to part with it when he came to retire and sell the rest of his farm.

"What's so interesting about Steinn Brothers? The locals don't like them. Some folk were extremely upset when they were granted permission to build there. We have no other industrial sites in that area, it's all farming. There was a lot of grumbling about back handers to councillors when the application was rushed through. In fact, it's rumoured the mayor bought a new Jaguar that very same week."

"I understand they develop and test drugs for the pharmaceutical industry; probably novel strains of antibiotics, treatments for tropical diseases and anti-rejection drugs for transplant surgery. They are licensed to clone tissue samples to use for the tests.

They must have a whole laboratory full of experimental animals. My sixth form students would benefit from visiting the real world of biology and seeing the theories put into practice."

Tony was surprised a newcomer should be so well informed. He had heard worrying rumours from some of the sixth form, who were keen anti-vivisectionists. They claimed the laboratories were testing noxious substances on living animals, but no one really knew what went on at the plant. Barry Dickinson, one of his sixth form history group, had tried to enlist his help to put up posters and deliver leaflets condemning the practices. The boy even had the cheek to glue a skull and crossboned animal rights sticker on the Sierra. It helped hide a bad patch of rust, but Tony had washed it off when the Headmaster sarcastically enquired if he was taking up piracy.

"I suppose your biology students have no objections to animal experiments?" He tried to imagine an advanced level biology course without dissections.

"There would be no new, life saving medicines if we couldn't test them on animals." Diana observed pragmatically.

After lunch, Tony drove them out to the pharmaceutical plant. The country roads were very quiet so he was surprised to meet a noisy crowd of young protesters blocking the slip road to the factory. A familiar figure waving a home made banner, leapt in front of the Sierra.

"Stop! Stop! You can't go in there, Mr Tompkins, sir." The placard was pushed at the windscreen.

Tony wound down his window. "Dickinson, Miss Scullery and I need to get into the plant to arrange a school visit. Kindly get out of our way. He leaned on the car horn and scattered the group as he accelerated through them, screeching to a halt only when he reached the barrier.

The security guard stepped out of his office, tilted back his head to peer at them suspiciously from under his peaked cap, and enquired gruffly what they wanted. A few words of explanation; a hurried phone call to his boss, and they were ushered into the visitors' reception area.

Inside the plush office, Diana arranged with the research director's secretary for a sixth-form visit. There were no problems when the secretary realised it was a visit from the biology class of the local school, for Steinn Brothers tried to court good publicity to counter the constant bad press it received from the Animal Rights campaigners.

"I suppose we will be able to see all your research facilities?"

"That's up to the director and security, but you definitely wont be allowed inside building 37. That's so secret even I'm not allowed in there," the secretary joked.

Tony stared down at the plush carpet, which was so deep the pile covered his shoe. He sank into a leather armchair set by a low, glass table, and picked up a glossy magazine. He felt slightly uncomfortable. The whole area reminded him of the lounge of an expensive hotel.

Tony had to admit Diana was extremely businesslike in her dealings with the secretary. She had obviously done this sort of thing many times before. He listened until he lost interest, as the detailed arrangements for the visit were finalised. To his mind, all these large industrial concerns were the same. They were scared stiff of competitors stealing their ideas or bound by the Official Secrets Act, because they undertook work for the government. That embargo on building 37 was typical of their attitude. They liked to pretend they had something worth hiding. As far as he could see they were all paranoid.

Chapter Four

Once they had run the gauntlet of animal rights supporters and left the Steinn Brothers' research plant behind them, Tony Tompkins drove the Sierra further along Beggars Bush Lane. He had decided to go another way home and take the scenic route back to town. Not that this other way was prettier than the one they had already used, but it was several miles longer and he was looking for an excuse to spend more time with Diana Scullery.

As he drove, Tony secretly pumped his foot up and down on the accelerator and occasionally tickled the brakes, making the car lurch about as if it was developing a fault. He had ideas to fake a breakdown on their way back, at some lonely spot in the countryside, to give him an opportunity to get to know his pretty companion much better.

The car lurched along the road beside the high, barbed wire fence, which protected the Steinn Brothers plant, and turned the corner to head towards Runford. Once clear of the industrial site, Diana noticed a dense stretch of woodland running alongside the security fence. Amongst the trees she caught sight of a painted sign declaring the area was a private nature reserve.

"Who owns that land? Is it the Lincolnshire Trust for Nature?" She turned and cast a professional eye over the plantation. "It looks like well-managed, mature, broadleaf woodland. Perhaps I could take some of my junior classes bird watching in there Maybe we could arrange a tree survey or a wildflower count." Turning to Tony she asked him, point blank. "Do you know who owns that wood?"

Tony pretended not to hear. That particular wood was his Uncle Albert's property, but the unfortunate episode in the pub, when the old fellow turned up in his dressing gown, was still fresh in his mind. He had no intention of reminding his pretty companion of the loony fringe to his family. He concentrated on his driving and ignored Diana's questions, hoping she would drop the subject. Unfortunately for Tony, the loony fringe to his family was very close at hand! A white-clad figure was clambering over the five bar gate out of the nature reserve just as the Sierra passed.

"Isn't that your uncle?" Diana shouted.

"Oh where? Surely not.? Perhaps it's just somebody who looks like him." Tony tried to stall for time, cursing his bad luck that the old fellow should be at that particular place at that precise moment. Ten seconds earlier and they would have missed him. If only they hadn't been delayed by those protestors.

That was one more valid reason to give Dickinson lots of extra homework next week.

"It is your Uncle Albert, and he's seen us."

"Oh! What a lucky coincidence. So it is." Tony braked to a halt, smiling through gritted teeth as he resigned himself to their bad timing.

Albert had recognised the Sierra. He stood in the road beside his pickup truck, waving his arms wildly in their direction, trying to attract their attention.

In his rear view mirror, Tony could see the old fellow was dressed in his white towelling dressing gown and mud covered gym shoes. Tony's heart sank down to the car's worn pedals. The silly old devil looked as if he was playing at druids again!

Albert seemed very excited. He ran to the car and rapped on the driver's window before Tony had time to wind it down.

"I'm glad I've seen you. I've just repeated that druidical ceremony, and it worked again!" From the breathless way he spoke and the joyous expression on his face, the two young teachers could have assumed Albert was studying alchemy and had just turned a ton of scrap metal into pure 24 carat gold!

"Hello again, Mr Williams. You look extra pleased with yourself." Diana leaned over and shouted from the passenger seat, struggling to make herself heard above the loud revving of the engine.

"So would you, missie; so would you, if you 'd just seen what I have," Albert replied enigmatically.

"Well, whatever it was you saw in your woods, I'm pleased for you." Even as he spoke Tony was still pumping the accelerator like a Grand Prix driver on the starting grid, preparing for a fast getaway. "Now, Diana and I must get back to town. So we'll say goodbye." He was about to wind up the car window and stamp on the accelerator when his uncle placed a restraining hand on the top rim of the glass and poked his head into the car. Tony knew he was beaten. He sighed and switched off the engine. Fate had decreed this would happen. He might have known Uncle Albert would pop out of the woodwork to plague him when all he wanted was to get to know Diana Scullery much better.

Diana obviously had no such reservations. In fact, she seemed very eager to jump out of the car and talk to the old man. She was out of the passenger seat and leaning over the gate staring into the woods before Tony could apply the handbrake and climb reluctantly out of his car. Somehow she seemed very taken with the old fellow. If Albert had been a younger man, Tony would have felt jealous. As it was, he felt the need to humour her, as he wanted to keep friendly with her.

"Do you get many wild birds in your woods? What about animals? What about wildflowers? Do you get any problems from being next to an industrial site?" She asked.

Albert smiled appreciatively. Here was someone who spoke his language and shared his interest in the wildlife. "We have tree creepers, lesser spotted woodpeckers; there's even a tawny owl nests here every spring. A vixen raised a litter of three cubs here last year. Are you interested in wild-life, young lady?"

"Do call me Di…Yes, I'm very interested. I teach biology and I was wondering if I could bring a group of my students bird watching."

Albert's expression changed abruptly. He hesitated and looked down at his muddy shoes. Pulling a long piece of grass from the hedgerow, slowly he chewed the fleshy end while he gave the request some thought. It was painfully obvious he had reservations about the idea of opening his woodland to schoolchildren. Eventually he replied, but he chose his words carefully.

"Usually I've no objections to a bit of education for the kids… especially about the countryside … but right now I'm not so sure. I'm carrying out my druid ceremonies, you see…" His voice trailed off into silence and he started to chew the grass again.

"I'd accompany them. I'm sure Tony would too." She shot an encouraging smile at the history teacher. "We'd make sure there was no damage. We'll insist they obey the countryside code."

"In the past, you've let the bird and mammal recorders in from the Natural History Society, haven't you, uncle?" Tony joined in, trying to persuade the old man to agree with Diana's suggestion. Tony wasn't interested in bird watching, not of the feathered varieties, but an outing like that would give him a legitimate excuse to get Diana into the woods.

"Aye. I used to … now I'm not so sure."

"What's changed, Uncle Albert? Has someone been vandalising the place?

"No, nothing like that." The old man's frown deepened as he wrestled with his thoughts. The two teachers waited patiently for him to continue. Finally he seemed to come to some sort of solution to his problem. He relaxed and smiled, putting his arm around his nephew's shoulder.

"Look here, I'd better let you into my secret." He climbed the gate and sat on the top bar, revealing a wide pair of khaki shorts under his white toga. His thin hairy legs stuck out of them like twin silver birch saplings from a pair of brown plant pots.

"You recall I mentioned in the pub how I'd been successful in one of my ceremonies? Well, I tried it again this morning. And it worked for me again!" Albert's lined face was wreathed in smiles as he spoke. It was proving impossible for him to conceal his excitement. "I'll tell you what happened, but you must swear to tell no one else about it."

"Scout's honour." Tony agreed reluctantly. This talk of druid ceremonies was ridiculous and sure to make him a laughing stock with Diana.

"You never were in the bloody Boy Scouts! They wouldn't have you after that funny business with those Girl Guides!"

"Oh alright! Cut my throat and hope to die! Now what is so damned important?" Tony blushed crimson at this reminder of his sordid past.

Without another word, Albert pulled a coloured Polaroid photograph from his pocket and handed it to his nephew.

"Good God! Have you been taking trick photographs in those woods?"

"I thought you'd say that, lad. I swear on the Sacred Mistletoe that's exactly as it happened. No tricks and no retouching. I took that very picture in these very woods, just half an hour ago."

Tony shook his head in disbelief and handed the colour picture to Diana. She was smiling politely when she took the print. Her expression changed to astonishment the instant she set eyes on it. "This is impossible! They don't exist in real life, surely? You've made it up!" She turned accusingly to the old man.

"What do you think it is then, young lady? You're a biologist, aren't you? You should know what it is, if anybody knows."

"It's a...it appears to be a...it looks exactly like a..."

" A Mythical beast!" Tony supplied the answer. "Some heraldic animal! A fairytale monster! It's a bloody Gryphon!" Turning on his uncle, he exclaimed. "Come on Uncle Albert, stop kidding us. It's a stuffed birds torso on a stuffed animal's body ... isn't it?"

Slowly Albert shook his head. From his serious expression, It was clear he was as puzzled as the young people.

"Show me where it was." Diana was through the gate before the two men could move.

Tony looked at her in astonishment. Surely she was joking? A biology graduate couldn't take this sort of thing seriously. She was being subtly sarcastic, or humouring the old chap. Against his better judgement, he decided he had better play along with the game if he wanted to keep in her good books.

Albert led the group as they made their way in single file through his woodland to the site of his discovery. They walked for several minutes and finally halted close by the barbed wire security fence that surrounded the Steinn Brothers research facilities. They came to a halt in a grassy glade, between two rows of oak trees.

"My druid grove." Albert explained proudly, waving his arms expansively in the air.

They could see the grass was still flattened where Albert had conducted his ceremony and where he had placed a single concrete paving slab to act as an altar.

"I made my sacrifice here." Albert pointed to the flat stone, which still had blood stains visible on it.

"What do you sacrifice?" Tony asked, aghast. This was a side to his uncle he had never suspected. Hair raising tales of human sacrifice came to his mind. As a history student, he had read Julius Caesar's account of the ancient druids carving up babies on their altars and burning their adult victims in baskets

"Don't look so upset, lad. I bought a rabbit from the butcher. It was already dead."

"Oh, I see. That's a relief."

"Tell me exactly what happened." Diana paced up and down the oak grove with the Polaroid picture clutched in her outstretched hand. She was trying to work out exactly where the camera had been placed to take the shot.

"I cut up the rabbit with my official bronze knife and placed it on that altar stone. I had finished my chants and was hiding among those beech saplings. That beast came from behind the largest oak and took the sacrifice, just as it did yesterday. Today though, I was prepared for the blighter. I had my camera at the ready."

Diana held up the photograph and compared the scene at the altar with the print in her hand. She checked and rechecked then shook her head in astonishment.

"Well?" Tony asked.

"He's right! Look here. You can see the Eagle's head and wings on a Lion's body. This is amazing! I always thought these heraldic animals were just fanciful ideas. This is stupendousThis will make international news. It would make a sensational article for Nature. The Natural History unit at Anglia or BBC Bristol would pay a fortune for this news." When she

33

saw Tony's mouth drop open she added, with a twinkle in her eyes. "It might even get on Blue Peter."

"Hang on one minute, Diana." Albert snatched the photograph from her hand. "I raised this mythical beast with my druid prayers. You are not going to write to the press or one of your new fangled scientific journals. And you definitely are not putting it on TV! No! I don't want hoards of reporters and thousands of anoraked twitchers tramping through my woods One more idea like that and I'll deny everything and burn this photograph."

Diana threw up her hands in frustration. "Don't do that! Please, Mr Williams. We must do more research. This whole thing is mind blowing!"

Albert closed his fingers around the photograph and pushed his hand firmly into his toga pocket.

Tony reviewed the situation rapidly. Much as he disbelieved what he was hearing, Diana seemed strangely ready to go along with the idea. He tried to soothe his uncle's fears. "We'll tell no one Just we three, uncle. It'll be our little secret. Isn't that right, Di?"

Diana let her breath out like a punctured balloon and nodded her head in what looked like reluctant agreement, but from the gleam in her eyes she wasn't too disappointed at the lack of publicity.

Tony reached out and prised the Polaroid photograph from his uncle's protective grasp, then he retraced Diana's steps and viewed the altar stone from the position used for the camera, checking it all for himself. There was no doubt about it. Something with an Eagle's head, feathered neck and wings, set on an animal's furry body, had taken the offering from the altar. The camera shutter had fired at the precise moment the hooked beak closed on the rabbit's leg. There was no double exposure and no other camera tricks he could detect. He knew a Polaroid print was produced inside the camera and without a negative, so there was no opportunity to fiddle with the picture in the processing. The trees and shrubs looked identical to the print in his hand. Anyway, his Uncle Albert was transparently honest, and as excited as a numerologist who'd just cracked the lottery. It was difficult for Tony to doubt him. He looked closer at the image on the photograph.

"A bit of a small Lion, wasn't it? Looks more the size of a young cub or even a dog, to me." The other two looked at the picture, compared it with the size of the paving slab and had to agree.

"By the looks of that tail, it might even be the back half of a bloody Whippet!" Tony muttered to himself. He peered around the wood nervously. It had just dawned on him that Eagles were fierce birds and Whippets could move like lightning. If this animal did exist, it was a worrying combination.

Diana seemed to have no such qualms. All she appeared to see was the interest to science. As she explained. "An animal, long regarded as a figment of the ancient's imagination, has come to life in Runford in the twenty first century. It will rock the scientific establishment."

Tony began to believe she was genuinely interested, but privately he was still suspicious of her motives. Maybe she was ambitious. Maybe, in her mind's eye, fame and a Doctorate beckoned.

"When do you intend to try your secret rites again, Uncle Albert?" she asked very sweetly.

Tony shrugged his shoulders at this sudden familiarity, recognising it as a transparent attempt to wheedle her way into the old man's confidence. If he hadn't fancied Di so much, he would have told her to cut out the flannel, but torn between lust and family loyalty, his hormones won the day. He decided to try and take the heat out of the situation.

"Surely there must be some mistake? Diana, you can't believe all this on the evidence of one out-of-focus Polaroid, can you?"

Albert frowned at his nephew. "You disbeliever! I have raised the beast twice now, and it's not out of focus. Would you like me to try a third time, with you two as witnesses?"

This was the last thing Tony wanted. He was about to deny any interest in the experiment, when Diana jumped at the offer.

"Shall we try now?"

Albert shook his head. "It's had one feed today. I don't suppose it'll be ready for another yet." His farming background and common sense had not entirely deserted him.

"Then, what about tomorrow?" She asked eagerly. "It's Sunday. Tony and I are not at work and the weather forecast sounds favourable."

Chapter Five

Sunday was the morning Tony Tompkins always lazed in bed until dinner time, recovering from the week at school and all the beer he'd consumed at the Duck and Dumplings on the Saturday night. That particular Sunday morning he surfaced early and crawled reluctantly out of bed as he had promised Diana Scullery he would accompany her and his Uncle Albert to Beggars Bush wood to try to repeat the druid ceremony.

"I must be mad! I must be absolutely mad..." He kept repeating that mantra to himself as he shaved, and later, as he chewed a bacon sandwich and stared blankly at the newspaper. "I must be completely mad! My one day off, and Di volunteers both of us to keep my crazy uncle company. I daren't tell my mum what he's up to this time."

He was just gulping down his third cup of black coffee when the doorbell rang. Diana stood on the step, hopping from one dainty foot to the other, looking as fresh as tomorrow's news, hyperactive and raring to go.

"Isn't it exciting, Tony? I'm so glad your uncle took us into his confidence. What if we actually get close enough to see this beast?"

Tony drained his cup, reluctantly threw on his jacket, and slouched out to join her.

"Don't forget your druid's robe," she reminded him.

He scowled. Uncle Albert had insisted they must dress as druids, if they wanted to take part in his ceremonial sacrifice. He had made some silly excuse about the vibrations and the orbs being affected. At the time, Tony had tried to protest, but Diana had just smiled sweetly and agreed readily. He thought she would have agreed to anything if it meant seeing that mythical creature. "It's a pity I didn't bribe Albert to tell her, a naked virgin is an essential part of the ritual," he thought ruefully. "Maybe next time." He went back upstairs and grabbed a grubby white bath towel from the rail before he followed Diana to his car.

There was not much traffic on the fen roads that morning. Tony had little to say. It took him all his powers of concentration to drive the car at that time on a Sunday. Diana was extra talkative and took the opportunity to ask Tony a favour as they drove to their meeting.

"I don't like the digs I've got myself, but I had to take what I could get when I first moved into Runford. Do you know of any nice accommodation? It'll have to be not too expensive and near the school.

He just nodded that he understood he request.

39

Diana continued. "I felt you would be the best person to ask, you being a local. I'd be very grateful…ever so grateful…" She smiled sweetly as if she was already in his debt.

Tony was flattered and excited at the thought of all that gratitude. He shook his tired brain into life and actually managed to answer her. "Let me put out a few feelers. I'm sure I can help."

When they arrived at the woods, Albert had already donned his white bathrobe and had unloaded the ceremonial props from his truck.

"Morning Tony. Morning Di. It's a nice day for it."

Tony grinned half-heartedly. It was indeed a nice morning for 'it'. If 'it' meant staying in bed or making passionate love to Diana Scullery, always assuming she could be persuaded to be that grateful. But, prancing about a wood, dressed up like refugees from a Turkish bath, was not his idea of fun. He glanced up and down the road in case any of his students were holding another early protest and they might spot him in his ridiculous fancy dress. Diana wrapped herself in her white robe; it was a passable little number she'd run up from an old sheet.

"What about yours, Tony?"

"I can't walk in it. I'll put it on when we get deep in the woods."

They walked in single file to the oak glade that Albert had designated his druid grove. All was quiet and normal. The old man placed the dead rabbit on the concrete altar slab then sharpened his crescent bladed bronze knife on the edge of the stone.

"Here, I've photocopied the hymn sheet so you can join in. With all three of us chanting, we might raise several of those rare animals."

Diana handed a copy to Tony.

"Must I?" He whispered, as he draped the damp bath towel over his shoulders, taking care to keep the obvious skid marks to the inside.

"Yes you must. Anyway, no one can see us here in the woods. So what are you worried about?"

Uncle Albert held up a bloodstained finger, demanding silence. "I will finish cutting up this sacrifice, then we must fall on our knees, face the East, and recite the incantations. Follow my example and you can't go wrong."

Tony shook his head in disbelief. But, under Diana's disapproving gaze, he did as he was told.

It took half an hour to complete the service. At last, Albert, in his capacity of Pollawsdoc the druid, raised his arms to the tall oak trees surrounding them. Shouting some unintelligible words, he fell flat on his face on the grass. Diana followed suit, giving Tony a warning glance over her shoulder, as she did so. He lowered himself onto his stomach and lie on the grass, trying to peer up her gown from his prone position.

There they lay, three hopeful people. Two pairs of eager eyes fixed on the dead rabbit. One lecherous pair gazing hopefully at the back of Diana Scullery's dimpled knees. The trees rustled gently overhead. No one spoke.

After some ten minutes, Tony developed cramp in his arms, which were spread above his head. The other two lay motionless with their eyes fixed on the altar. Tony was about to get up and declare the whole fiasco over. His discomfort was becoming unbearable, and Diana had kept her legs tightly together and her modesty intact. Suddenly Albert hissed a warning call for silence.

"Shush!"

From nearby there came the unmistakable flutter of wings. Cramp in muscles and cheap thrills were forgotten in the excitement of that unique moment. Diana held her breath. She stared unblinking at the stone slab. Albert moved very slowly to cock his camera shutter and repeated the last lines of the incantation under his breath. Even Tony tore his eyes from Diana's legs and focused his undivided attention on the sliced rabbit.

The wingbeats came closer. A bird or something similar could be heard rustling among the trees. Suddenly, with a loud flutter of flight feathers, a large black shape settled on the blood stained carcass.

"Damn carrion crow!" Albert exclaimed, rising to his knees and brandishing his bronze knife at the feathered thief.

Tony burst into giggles at the sudden release of tension. He rolled over on his back and stared up into the canopy of oak leaves. This was a farce, just as he had anticipated it would be. It was definitely not worth the inconvenience of getting out of bed before noon on a Sunday. He squinted at the patterns formed by the sun filtering through the leaves. They reminded him of the green patterned curtains in his spare room. He suddenly remembered Diana's request for some new digs. It struck him, if he cleared out his books and the old cricket gear, that spare back bedroom would make a cosy accommodation for a young lady lodger. The possibility of Diana sleeping under the same roof excited him. He almost shared his idea with her right then, but thought better of it. Perhaps I'd better get it cleaned and wallpapered before I mention it to her, he thought.

The trio was subdued and silent as they returned to the road and their vehicles. The failed attempt to raise the fabulous beast had been a disappointment; at least to Albert and Diana. Tony had always been very sceptical. Their walk back through the woods to the main road was completed in silence. They hardly managed to raise a word of greeting when Muldoon jogged past the car, on one of his regular keep fit runs.

Half an hour later, in the pub, the three of them sat at a corner table and discussed the morning. This time, no one took any notice of them. Tony and Diana had sensibly left their makeshift robes in his car and Albert had remembered to change into his normal clothes before he drove back to town. Obviously, the rude comments he had suffered on the previous occasion had taught him to be more discreet.

"I don't understand it." Albert shook his head sadly.

"I do." Tony said belligerently. "There never was a fairytale beast. You copied that photo from some child's comic or a library book on Myths and Legends."

Diana jumped to the old man's defence. "No. I still believe Uncle Albert. Today things were just not right for an appearance."

Tony couldn't believe his ears. This was an educated biologist speaking! He put down his beer glass. "What do you mean, 'an appearance'? That was not the London Palladium, you know."

"I mean, the vibes or something were not quite right."

Albert nodded vigorous agreement. "It's you, Tony my boy. You didn't believe. It was your hostile and unclean thought waves. That's what made us fail."

Silently, Tony conceded the possibility. His thoughts about Diana were certainly not the purest as he lay behind her on the grass, staring up her toga, hoping for a glimpse of her panties. He felt suddenly uncomfortable and glanced furtively up from his beer. Surely the old man had no way of knowing what he'd been thinking? An experienced mystic might be able to read people's minds, but this was only his Uncle Albert. He put aside his fears and was about to declare his innocence when he remembered Diana was firmly on Albert's side in this business. With no wish to antagonise her, he swallowed his protests, nodded silent agreement and returned to supping his beer.

"What will you do now?" Diana asked.

"I will write a report to the Archdruid in Macclesfield, asking for his help. Free advice is included in the original fee. It says so in the prospectus." He pulled the dog-eared manuscript from his pocket and ran his finger along the bottom of the page to where the guarantee mentioned that fact. It was written in very small letters just above the declaration in large red print. 'This document is the property of the Druids of the Mystic Mistletoe Co Ltd. That sounded more like a branch of Woolworth than a religious organisation. Tony looked up to the bar ceiling and shook his head in despair before he drained his beer glass to hide his true feelings.

Chapter Six

"What do you mean, Smiffy. 'The Eagle-dog has flown'? Have you been watching those war videos again? Only last week you were raving about 'The Eagle has Landed.'"

"I caught that hybrid flying around its exercise cage behind building 37, Mr Armstrong. When I went in to feed and water it, it was flapping its wings and hovering above my head."

The head keeper slid back his peak cap and frowned at his underling. He scratched the back of his thick neck, digesting the bad news. If that beast escaped they would both be for the high jump.

"Get a net put over the top of that outdoor cage at once, and don't mention this to anyone, especially the research boffins. If this gets back to Dr Steinn, I wouldn't want to be within five hundred miles of here."

John Armstrong walked back to his office and sat down heavily at his desk. He sighed like a man with the world's problems on his back. It was enough of a strain being responsible for Steinn Brothers' experimental livestock, without the damn specimens escaping. These hybrids needed very special attention. He was sick of preparing their special diets, keeping their cages at optimum temperature, measuring their fluid intake, and ensuring they ate the correct dosage of the drugs supplied by the research department. He'd never had this trouble when he worked at Children's Corner at Skegness Zoo.

Monitoring the Eagle-dog's bodily functions for any signs of problems was very time consuming. Now it appeared the creature could fly. That meant it might even escape! God! If the national newspapers or the licensing authorities got wind of what they were doing here, the boss would go spare. It wasn't just the matter of losing his job that worried him. Dr Frank Steinn, head of research, was not a man to cross. Armstrong was a big man but he was genuinely afraid of his boss. He shuddered at the thought of it. There was a knock on the office door.

"Another thing, Mr Armstrong. That Eagle-dog hasn't eaten its food again today."

"What do you mean, 'again'?"

"It didn't eat it yesterday, either."

"Oh Lord! That means it's been two days without its drugs. Now I'll have to tell Dr Steinn. But, we'll have no mention of flying. OK, Smiffy?" Armstrong dismissed Roland Smith, the under keeper, and telephoned the research director's office. He was relieved to find Dr Steinn was out and glad to leave a message with his secretary, instead of explaining the problem to him personally.

It was mid-afternoon on Monday before Dr Steinn returned to the Runford research laboratories. He had been at a board meeting in London on the Friday afternoon and had stayed at his brother's flat in Knightsbridge for the weekend. The Steinn brothers were majority shareholders in Steinn Chemicals, the parent companyDr Frank Norman Steinn was head of research, his older brother, Arnold, was company chairman. The rest of the board consisted of elderly aunts and cousins who never interfered with the running of the business. They were all genuine sleeping partners. There was a token Member of Parliament, who was a non-executive director, but he never attended business meetings, and only put in one appearance a year at the office party, with the sole purpose of picking up some young female secretary for the night. The Honourable Member was content to receive a fat fee in used notes, sealed in the obligatory brown paper envelope, for lobbying the corridors of power on behalf of the Steinn company. The Steinn brothers were unhindered by nosy shareholders. They did pretty well exactly as they pleased.

Frank Steinn had made the Runford plant his personal responsibility. He treated the biological research department as if it were his private toy, using the facilities to further his own dreams. The programme to develop cross species hybrids was his main preoccupation and he pursued it relentlessly, even to the point of ignoring the tight laws governing such contentious experiments.

"Armstrong! Armstrong! Where the bloody hell are you, man?" Dr Frank Steinn stalked into building 37, his foul mood etched all over his bloated red face.

The head keeper threw down his bucket and raced to his boss' side.

"What do you mean, 'the Eagle-dog has refused to take its daily dose'? You've fed it, haven't you? It likes the mix we use, doesn't it? In tests, nine out of ten Whippets said they preferred it. Damn it all! The beast should be hungry, considering the small amount of food we give it."

"It's left its food for two days now, sir."

"Good God!" Steinn cursed. "This is impossible. How can I control its growth pattern if you fail to do your job properly?"

"I've saved the food to show you, sir."

"Damn me! I've no wish to inspect a dried up saucer of pet food, you idiot! Follow me." The irate doctor stormed into Armstrong's office to check the written feeding records. He found his worse fears were confirmed.

"We'll have to get close to it and inject the drugs. You get a lamb bone or something similar from the staff canteen to tempt it. That should appeal to both halves of the belligerent hybrid."

"Do you want me to dip the food in the drugs, sir?"

"No, Armstrong! Don't be stupid! I need to be sure the creature gets the full dose. You will entice it into a corner then pop this falconry hood over its head."

"What about the Whippet half, sir? Will a simple leather hood work efficiently, as it's half dog?"

"Oh alright, man! Put a bloody dog muzzle on the beak as well, if you think it will help. I don't mind what you do, as long as you immobilise it long enough for me to inject it."

The head keeper left in a hurry, pleased to be away from his boss and the Eagle-dog. He headed for the staff canteen.

Dr Steinn walked over to the Eagle-dog's cage and admired his creation through the wire mesh. This specimen was one of his outstanding successes. In the past he had created surgically his nightmare creatures by joining living bits together. Of course the rejection rate was high and few survived for long. He had made rat-rabbits and hamster-mice, but Professor Enrico Steinn, his brilliant uncle in Florence, had carried out the unique operation of joining two eggs together. He had taken genetic material from an Eagle and a dog, and managed to fertilise the result. Once that tricky bit was done they had muggled the embryo to England, to the Steinn Brothers Runford plant for development. The resulting specimen was half bird and half mammal. Compound 104, their latest and most powerful hybridisation and cloning aid, had ensured the embryo recovered from the radical technique and actually thrived. It also ensured the two halves of the creature's physical makeup developed at the same rate. This was the breakthrough he had been working for.

"If I can create a mythical beast like a Grypho, well something resembling a Gryphon..." he muttered to himself, remembering the original heraldic beast was half Eagle and half Lion, but they couldn't obtain Lion ova and had had to make do with some from a Whippet....The possibilities are endless. With Enrico's technique and our money and facilities, it will be like the game of 'Heads and Tails' my brother and I used to play as children. If I can imagine it, I can make it! We could supply centaurs to the racing fraternity or winged warriors to the RAF. My God! But there's a fortune to be made here. I'm a genius."

Of course, pushing forward the frontiers of hybridisation procedures was his personal dream. But there was one small problem. This type of experiment was strictly illegal in the UK. The powers that be frowned on anyone undertaking unauthorised experiments. The government had put in place a stringent licensing system for such undertakings, especially after the development of Dolly the cloned sheep. There was no way he could get permission to create monsters like this. If the government agencies found out, he knew he could finish up behind bars.

"I couldn't help overhearing, Sir. There's no need to muzzle the poor beast." Smiffy the under keeper, broke into Dr Steinn's thoughts.

"Eh? What do we do then to make the animal take its medicine?"

"I get on well with it, sir. If you let me in the cage it will calm down. It trusts me."

"Trusts you, does it? How is it you think you can do better than Armstrong?"

"I've always fed it and looked after it, sir. It's my baby...so to speak. Anyway, I'm used to birds and dogs. My dad used to breed greyhounds and me mum keeps chickens. Let me show you." Smiffy opened the cage and talked gently to the Eagle-dog. The hybrid calmed down and let the keeper stroke its neck. He gently ruffled the sleek black feathers and smoothed them down again, then he patted the fur on the dog's back and spoke in a calm low voice. "Come on old chap. No one is going to harm you. You know old Smiffy wouldn't do you any harm."

The creature rubbed itself against his leg and made a sound in its throat like a contented eagle.

"Right." Dr Steinn joined the keeper in the cage and approached the Eagle-dog, but the creature backed away from him, trying to hide behind the keeper's legs.

"Hold it still, man!" Steinn held the syringe aloft, the gleaming needle pointing upwards towards the top of the enclosure. The Eagle/ dog panicked.

"Begging your pardon, sir, but if you give that to me I will inject the dog in its rump."

Dr Steinn held his hands up in a gesture of resignation and handed the loaded syringe to Smiffy, who gently but firmly held the back half of the hybrid and injected the drug into a large thigh muscle, with no fuss at all.

"There you are then. Good boy. You'll feel better for that." Smiffy soothed the creature as he massaged the injection site with his fingers.

Dr Steinn and Smiffy had just backed out of the cage when Armstrong arrived on the scene, triumphantly holding a cooked chicken leg in his hand.

"You're too late, Armstrong. Thanks to your assistant here, we have given the creature its drugs." Turning to Smiffy the doctor smiled encouragingly. "That was a good job. Well done, Smith. I shall not forget your expertise in this matter."

Smiffy blushed crimson and bent his head to hide his embarrassment under the peak of his cap.

When Steinn had gone and everything was back to normal, Armstrong tackled his underling about the incident.

"You trying to take my job, or something? What's your little game, Smiffy?"

"No, chief. Honest. I just couldn't bear to see the Eagle-dog upset. I've looked after it since it was a young un and I know it trusts me."

Armstrong couldn't argue with that. He was just a bit frightened of the creature and had gladly allowed Smiffy to take charge of it. Rather him than me, he thought gratefully. That bloody great beak could tear your eyes out if the creature took a dislike to you!

Absentmindedly he nibbled on the chicken leg and went back to his desk.

Chapter Seven

There was an uneasy atmosphere in The Duck and Dumplings. The regulars were crowded together at one end of the bar. Paddy Murphy, the barman, occupied the centre ground, standing alone behind the polished counter in splendid isolation. At the other end of the bar, nearest to the entrance, stood a solitary, dark stranger.

"Who is he?" Old Bob rasped in a stage whisper that echoed like a full-blown shout in the still of the room.

Paddy shook his head vigorously, put a finger to his lips and shot a warning glance at the pensioner, in a vain attempt to silence him.

"He looks like a civil servant to me. All dolled up in a waistcoat, black jacket and pinstripe trousers, with a briefcase at his side. That bowler hat and little toothbrush moustache remind me of somebody." Bob shuddered visibly. In the Lincolnshire fens very few men would draw attention to themselves by dressing so formally. Maybe in the city such behaviour would pass without comment but not in Runford, and certainly not in the Duck and Dumplings on a Thursday morning.

The stranger had stalked into the bar as Paddy was stocking the back shelves with bottled lager and soft drinks. The barman turned quickly at the sound of a strange voice.

"I'll have a small glass of non-alcoholic lemonade, my man." The newcomer spoke in a broad, northern accent, ignoring the curious stares of the locals.

"Well, he's certainly not from London," Bob observed. "But he has got a leather briefcase. I bet he's a taxman or a vat inspector. Perhaps he's one of them government Social Security snoops!" The entire group shuffled further down the bar, packing themselves into a small space beside the jukebox, like sardines in an upright tin.

"Of course, he might just be an undertaker on his holidays," someone murmured hopefully.

Paddy crossed himself religiously at the thought of a funeral director in his bar, dressed in dark mourning clothes. He poured out the soft drink and placed it on the drip mat in front of the mysterious stranger.

The man in the bowler hat scanned the room, his mean eyes peering from under the dark rim. Waving a crisp twenty pound note under Paddy's nose, he enquired. "Does Albert Williams drink in here? Are you expecting him in today?"

Everybody heard the request, but no one chose to answer. Paddy knew he would never tell. He had too much to hide about himself, but what about the others? They wouldn't snitch on a friend, not even for money? Or would they? The silence was almost tangible.

Old Bob cleared his throat noisily. The vision of several free pints of beer for information given, had just penetrated through to his devious mind. Paddy shot him a blistering glance, daring him to speak out of turn. That single stare held the promise of a lifetime's ban from the pub, at the very least. The pensioner reconsidered his position, lowered his head and sipped his near empty pint. The urge to speak passed. Reliefm rippled through the cramped ranks.

"I don't think we even know an Albert Wilkins. Do we?" Paddy stared at the regulars, daring anyone to contradict him.

The stranger grunted. "It's Albert Williams, not Wilkins. When he wrote to me, he told me he called in here every morning at about this time."

There was a stunned silence. Albert must be losing his marbles! Who but a lunatic would tell a tax inspector where to find him? Paddy shook his head in disbelief, but he did remember how Albert had been acting rather strangely of late. There was that one recent occasion when the old chap had arrived looking as if he had come straight from his bath. He had worn his coat over a towelling dressing gown and running shoes, but had forgotten to put on his trousers!

The street door swung open. Like the turkey invited to Xmas dinner, Albert Williams swaggered nonchalantly into his local, whistling cheerfully

All eyes turned towards the new arrival, moved back to the tax inspector, then finally focused pleadingly on the bar man. The cowardly Irishman chose to ignore their pleas. He dodged beneath the counter top like a publican in an old cowboy film; when the sheriff walks through the swing doors of the saloon straight into an armed ambush!

Albert, oblivious to these undercurrents, smiled at his cronies, nodded pleasantly towards the bowler hatted stranger, and sat down on a stool at the centre of the bar.

"Pint of your best bitter, Paddy," he ordered cheerfully.

The bar man shot up from his hiding place and pulled the pint very slowly. As he worked the beer pump, he attempted to attract Albert' s attention by nodding his head towards the stranger and rolling his bloodshot eyes towards towards the door.

"You feeling OK? I'm worried about you lately, Paddy, twitching like that. And you've developed red eye. You should lay off the hard stuff," Albert joked.

"He's alright, it's you we're all worried about, Albert Williams." Old Bob muttered distinctly. Judas could not have timed it better! The silence of fear was profound. You could have cut the air in the bar with a cheesewire. No one moved. No one dared to draw a breath. Time was suspended in mid tick. A bluebottle roared in through the window and landed noisily on the gin optic.

"Would you be Albert Williams the acolyte?" The tension was broken by a deep northern voice. The taxman held out his hand to Albert. "I'm Modnoc, the priest."

"Albert slid his glass along the polished counter towards the stranger, smiled broadly and enthusiastically pumped the podgy, outstretched hand.

"Come and sit where we can talk in private." Albert led his new friend to the far corner of the room.

"Well I'll be damned! What do you think of that, Paddy? Has Albert turned Queen's evidence or state informer, and shopped the lot of us?" Old Bob voiced all their fears. The bar man, who had worked in strip clubs and bingo halls and was much more worldly-wise than his country customers, shrugged his shoulders noncommittally. He kept his face straight and his emotions under tight control for he had more to lose than most of them. He was working full time at the pub and still claiming unemployment benefit, and he had two wives and four children back in the Emerald Isle. Behind his implacable mask the bar man's mind went into overdrive. Would the old fellow shop him? Should he make a run for it, by the back door, while there was still time? Inertia won. He decided he would have to trust Albert Williams until proved wrong, but being a gambling man with a penchant for each way bets, he propped open the bar hatch for a quick getaway. Then, just to be on the safe side, he kept his eyes glued on the ill-assorted pair in the far corner of the room.

Albert and his new friend shook hands solemnly, twisting their fingers in a most peculiar way as they greeted each other. It had to be some contrived secret signal and it was not wasted on the bar man.

"Freemasons?" He whispered to himself. "No, they don't keep their thumbs up like that." His quick mind went back to Albert's theatrical debut in his dressing gown. What was it he had announced on that occasion? Something about being a druid, wasn't it? Paddy went to place a freshly polished glass under the counter but he was so preoccupied spying on Albert and the taxman, he completely missed the shelf. The pint tankard crashed to the floor, splintering noisily on impact. The sudden noise woke up the entire room. Old Bob, overcome with nerves, laughed out loud even though his glass was empty. Everyone else took the breakage as a welcome sign to return to normality.

"What about the fine weather forecast for the weekend? We'll all be able to do outdoor jobs."

"Go for a walk by the river."

"Sure but it's no good for fishing." Paddy commented knowingly. He liked to sound knowledgeable on these matters, even though he'd never fished in his life. He would have spoken as easily on the Royal Family, sex shops, or the price of spring onions, if he felt his customers required it. He regarded well-informed chatting as part of his job description.

The two conspirators in the corner were forgotten and left in peace to talk privately to each other.

"Thank you for coming so quickly, Archdruid."

"The least I could do, in the circumstances." Modnoc the priest assured his newest acolyte. "Now, about this photograph." Under cover of the table, he slipped a photocopy of Albert's Polaroid print from his briefcase, slid it face down along the tabletop and flipped it over, with the dexterity of a card dealer in a casino. Albert glanced at the picture of the beast and grinned proudly.

"Tell me about this. I know you wrote me a full report, but this is most unusual. I need to know absolutely everything there is to know."

Albert detailed his escapade in Beggar Bush wood, leaving nothing unsaid. "I bought a fresh rabbit at the butchers and used the bronze sickle you provided with my first lesson. I couldn't get any Mistletoe. The florist said there was no call for it in the summer. She suggested watercress would serve as well, but I found a piece of plastic Mistletoe left over from a Christmas decoration…"

Modnoc listened attentively. Sometimes he nodded agreement. Often he shook his head or frowned when he needed clarification on some point.

"…I set up my altar facing east. I used a compass to be sure. I wore a white robe, specially washed at the launderette. And I recited the whole ceremony out loud… Did I mention, I bought a skinned rabbit from the butchers for the sacrifice?…"

At the end of his trainee's monologue, the Archdruid stroked his chin thoughtfully. There were two ways of looking at this phenomenon.

Either he had a complete nutter on his books, or something mysterious and wonderful had actually occurred. He eyed the old man across the pub table. The old fellow seemed sane enough on the surface. But then, he thought, he did pay my full fee without argument, so he can't be too bright.

"What do you think?" Albert asked eagerly.

"I think you'd better show me your oak grove and altar stone before I catch the evening train back to Macclesfield. This could prove to be a winner." Modnoc was indeed enthusiastic. It was the silly season in the newspapers and he was eager to get all the details before he sold the sensational story to one of the national dailies.

Chapter Eight

Archdruid Modnoc paced the length of the oak grove in Beggars Bush Wood, clutching his copy of the beast's photograph in his chubby fist. The man looked more out of place there in his dark business suit, polished shoes and bowler hat, than Albert had ever been, visiting the pub in his dressing gown and running shoes.

"You say the photograph was taken from over there?"

"Right here."

"It's a pity you didn't have an expensive camera. This print could be a lot sharper."

Albert shrugged his shoulders. The animal was fully visible and there was no mistaking its shape. Considering the circumstances he was pleased with the result.

"This picture would not reproduce well in newsprint. There's not enough definition or contrast. Do you have the original?"

"Newsprint!" Albert recoiled at the spectre of unwanted publicity. He wanted his name and his woods kept strictly private.

Modnoc detected the antagonism and added hastily. "I feel sure you will have no objections to me advertising your outstanding success in our monthly newsletter… and, of course, in our new colour prospectus. It'll be a great honour for you. My other druids will be very envious. It will drum up more business…sorry, I mean… many more acolytes will feel compelled to join us. You will be helping to spread the word."

"I'm not so sure about that…" Albert started to protest.

Modnoc went into top gear on his selling spiel. "I'll recompense you, of course. I'll put your name on our roll of honour; completely free of charge of course. Maybe we could supply you with our Advanced Chanting modules at half price. I could negotiate a 10% discount for you at Gowns R Us."

By then, Albert was full of doubts. He eyed the stranger thoughtfully. This natty city gent was hardly his idea of an Archdruid. He wore no ceremonial gown, no suitable head-dress, nor did he carry a staff or crozier. Surely a respected religious leader should look more mystical than a tubby bank clerk. On reflection, it struck Albert that Modnoc resembled Oliver Hardy from the cinema comedy duo! With comedians in mind, another interesting thought occurred to him.

"How do you spell your name?"

The Archdruid frowned; this fellow was unpredictable. "It's spelled M.O.D.N.O.C. Exactly as it sounds."

Albert reversed the spelling in his mind and grinned. "With a name like that, you must wonder if you're coming or going! Tell me, do you suffer from some kind of rubber fetish? Do strangers ever tell you to get knotted?"

Modnoc looked extremely puzzled. He frowned and shook his head.

Albert grinned even more. The fellow doesn't even know he's a backward condom, he thought gleefully. Fancy using a compromising name like that and not knowing it. Then an awful possibility struck him.

"How do I know you are who you claim to be? You could be an impostor! If you are the true Archdruid of Macclesfield, and the man who gave me my druid name, you would have understood my comments, just now."

Modnoc looked flushed and stared shiftily at the fresh mud on the toes of his shiny shoes. Finally he looked Albert straight in the eye and confessed. "I didn't actually choose your name. Pollawsdoc was the title suggested to me by my predecessor. He was the original Archdruid and the founder of our order. He supplied me with a list of names... He also named me."

"You're not the original Archdruid? I still don't understand. Explain it to me properly." Albert demanded, his hackles rising.

"I purchased the company from the original Archdruid when the old chap retired. It was a going concern and I invested my redundancy money from the bank. I picked your name from the list of acolyte titles he suggested to me."

"You mean you are not a trained druid? You don't have mystical powers?"

"I am the majority shareholder of the Druids of the Mystic Mistletoe Co Ltd. My wife owns the other 49%. That gives me all the power I require."

"You're a bloody fake! You know less than I do about the religion!"

"If what you say is true, how come you raised a mythical beast using my company's paperwork?" Modnoc snorted angrily.

Albert was stumped by this argument. Whether the potent incantations were the work of this bowler hatted twit or his predecessor was not the question. Maybe the first Archdruid knew what he was on about. The ceremony had produced outstanding results. That was what really mattered. Guardedly he said. "I'll have my picture back, if you don't mind. It's my property and you've no right to keep it."

"That's where you're wrong, Pollawsdoc. If you read the small print of our agreement, you'll find I keep sole rights in all the sacred works. You have no right to copy them or use them without the company's consent. You'll also find that any incidental profit made from my course is forfeit to the company... For the word 'company', read me...and of course, my dear wife. That mythical beast could be worth a lot of money and I have first rights to it." Modnoc thrust the photograph in his pocket and stuck out his chin aggressively, as he continued lecturing Albert. "I didn't invest my redundancy payment from Barclays bank in the Mystic Mistletoe Co Ltd, for any religious reasons. Oh no! It was done solely as a business venture. I did it for the money, just like any other established church!"

Albert stalked off angrily. He left His Holiness the Archdruid of Macclesfield standing in the middle of the oak grove in Beggars Bush wood. The impostor could find his own way back to Runford railway station.

Chapter Nine

Tony Tompkins was not good at wallpapering, or for that matter, at any household chores, especially cleaning up after himself. His mother called every week to tidy his terraced house and collect his dirty washing.

"I think it's a good idea of yours to share with a fellow teacher," Freda assured her son. "Tell me, what's his name?"

"Di, the new biology teacher. Started this term." Tony was deliberately brief, telling her as little as he could and avoiding any mention that his proposed lodger was a girl.

"I like Welsh lads, especially if they play Rugby," Freda said as she put his clean shirts in the wardrobe and his soiled clothes into a bag. She walked into the bathroom.

"I don't know how you get your bath towels so dirty. Anyone would think you'd be rolling on grass in this one." She cast her eyes over the spare room. "I'll pick up six rolls of wallpaper and get them hung later this week. You must sort out all these old books and your other rubbish. I'm sure there's a perfectly nice carpet under there somewhere. Will you be needing to hire a skip?"

Tony deliberately ignored his mother's error over Diana's name and sex. He frowned at the thought of tidying the spare room. Perhaps the idea of moving the girl in with him, was going to be just too much work. For a second he wondered if he'd made the right decision, but he realised he had little real choice now that his mother had taken to the idea with enthusiasm. In the long run, it would be worth it, he assured himself. In such a small house he would see an awful lot of Diana Scullery. Bumping into her in the bathroom, on the landing, in the kitchen, and hopefully in her bedroom.

At mid day he took Diana out to lunch and tentatively broached the subject with her.

"You know you mentioned getting a new flat as your present one isn't up to much. Would you object to sharing a house with one other teacher?"

"That sounds ideal. Have you thought of somewhere already? Is she a friend of yours?"

"What about a male teacher?"

Diana smiled and shrugged her shoulders. "I shared with two chaps at Uni. I can cope with that."

"Right, that's settled. I'll get my spare bedroom redecorated. You can move in next week."

"Are you asking me to move in with you, Tony?"

"What if I am? I have a spare room. You need new digs, and we get on well, don't we?"

She smiled knowingly. "As long as you realise it's only a business arrangement."

"Of course. What else?" He crossed his fingers under the cover of the table and lowered his head so his hair hid his face. His self-satisfied smirk was only visible to the mushy peas on his plate. That settled it. He'd call at the ironmongers on his way home and buy the other equipment he needed.

Tony's mother was a very organised woman. By the time he arrived home from work, she had piled all his rubbish on the landing, stripped the spare room down to the bare plaster and had hung the first three rolls of new wallpaper.

"I've made you a meat pie for your tea." She shouted down the stairs, as soon as she heard him open the front door and cross the hall. "When you are free, I need to have a word with you about your Uncle Albert."

Tony ate his pie and marked a bundle of the sixth form's history assignments. The last essay was Barry Dickinson's, the animal rights enthusiast. Tony was still peeved with the boy's actions at the Steinn Brothers plant so he deliberately dropped a blob of ketchup onto the centre page and closed the exercise book to spread the red mark even further. Then he wrote a cutting comment about producing such untidy work. He sat and drank the last dregs of his tea as he pondered over how much he need reveal about Albert's latest craze, when he spoke to his mother.

"Are you finished yet, Anthony? I'm waiting for you." The call came from the room above and it sounded ominous. His mother always reverted to his full name when she meant business.

"Coming, mum." Warily he climbed the stairs to the spare room and leaned against the doorframe, watching her apply paste to the strips of wallpaper with vigour.

"Were you by any chance, in the pub when your uncle came in, dressed in his dressing gown?" Freda never did mince her words when she was sure of her ground. It was obvious she must have heard about the incident, so it was no use Tony pretending he knew nothing.

"Yes, as a matter of fact, Di and I were having a quiet drink together."

"Is it true then? Did he announce yet another religious craze to those drinking cronies of his?" She paused in her pasting and stood with her hands lodged aggressively on her hips, the paste brush dangling between her fingers.

Tony had seen that steely glint in her eyes many times before. It always meant trouble. He shifted uneasily from one foot to the other and weighed his words very carefully.

"He was doing no harm, Mum. You didn't mind him being a Buddhist. Well, now he's a Druid. It's much the same sort of thing."

"Hmm!" She grunted her disapproval. "Why go out in public in his dressing gown?"

71

"Maybe he's getting absent minded?" Tony suggested.

"I think it's time my brother got himself a good woman to look after him. It's time he had a wife. A responsible wife would soon sort out all this religious nonsense. I'm going to have a word at the WI. There are one or two eligible widows among the members. I'll fix him up with the right sort of partner, you see if I don't."

Tony couldn't believe his ears. Uncle Albert finally married off! At his age! He was so shocked at the idea, his shoulder slipped off the door frame and he fell with a thud against the wall, noisily knocking the air out of his lungs.

"You alright, Anthony? Not sickening for something, are you?"

"No, mother. Just preoccupied with the thoughts of marking those History essays." He made a mental note to warn Albert of his fate the very next time he saw him.

Once Mrs Tompkins had completed the wallpapering and had gone home, Tony unpacked his purchases from the ironmongers and went into the newly decorated bedroom. He checked the partition wall, which divided Diana's room from his own, then he chose a dense patch of the floral pattern at head height. Taking care not to leave any telltale marks on the fresh wallpaper, he drilled a small hole through the wall into his own room.

"Its lucky for me mum chose a pattern with those small rose buds in it. They'll make the lens completely invisible." He was pleased with his work.

Once he had checked where the hole came through in his own room, he screwed in the door spy lens he had bought from the ironmongers, then he went into his own bedroom to check the result. Back in his own room he realised the object lens was clearly visible against the white expanse of his painted wall.

"Damn! I hadn't thought of that. It might be practically invisible in next door but anyone coming in here will notice my spy hole." Tony looked around his bedroom, searching for some way to hide the conspicuous lens.

"Ah! The wardrobe." He pushed his wardrobe along the wall to cover the evidence. Lying on his bed, he considered what he had achieved. He had a way of observing Diana without her seeing him. He could watch her dress and undress, but as it stood, he would have to move the wardrobe every time he wanted to spy on her. Apart from being hard work, with the weight of all his clothes in there, it would make a noise each time he moved it. With the wall being so thin, she was sure to hear the movement and she might get suspicious. Suddenly Tony had another brainwave.

"Why not get inside the ruddy wardrobe and use it as a hide. After all, it is bird watching!"

Ten minutes later he had drilled a hole in the back of his wardrobe and found he could stand inside that piece of furniture and peer through the lens into the next door bedroom. He punched the air in delight when he checked the view and realised he could see most of the room, with the exception of the door and the dividing wall. Unfortunately he got his fist tangled up in his collection of neckties and almost fell over inside the wardrobe.

Once he had disentangled himself he realised his plans were a success. Now he must ensure the bed in the spare room was pushed against the opposite wall, so that Diana would be in the middle of his field of view. He rubbed his hands together in anticipation of the erotic pleasures to come.

Chapter Ten

Head animal keeper John Armstrong, stirred his morning mug of tea with a ginger biscuit and opened his copy of the Sun. He eyed his assistant across the table and decided to skip the page three, topless pinup, saving her for later when he would be alone. He turned straight to the centre spread of news stories.

"Good God, Smiffy!" The head keeper's boots slipped off the table and he fell off his swivel chair onto the floor.

"You OK, boss?" Roland Smith, the under keeper, rushed around the desk and helped him up.

"No. I'm not bloody alright! Look in this damn newspaper!" He wiped the tea and soggy biscuit from the wet newspaper and spread the pages on his desk.

Smiffy smiled at the news. "That's our Eagle-dog, ain't it? He's a beauty. We'll all be famous now."

"Famous! Famous? We'll be lucky to stay alive when Dr Steinn sees this."

With this warning ringing in his ears, Smiffy peered closer at the photograph. "It's not very clear, is it. It looks more like a Lion than a Whippet cross. Look at them claws. They've been added in. Pr'aps it's all a fake. Could it be they're only guessing?"

"There's no smoke without fire. Look here at this report. It says … 'Somewhere in the fens of deepest Lincolnshire there is devil worship… Fabulous beasts are being brought back to life… Black magicians are raising these demons to feed on the blood of innocent children'".

"Well …there you are then. This is a scientific research establishment, not a witchcraft centre. And the Eagle-dog eats tins of dog food. Don't it?"

"But it mentions the Lincolnshire fens! There's no smoke without fire."

"I wouldn't worry. I can't see old Steinn reading today's Sun or any other day's Sun for that matter. He takes the Financial Times and a load of scientific journals, from what his secretary tells me."

"All the same, you and I are on Red Security Alert until further notice. Not one whisper to anybody about this." The head keeper screwed up his unread paper and stuffed it into the waste bin, all thoughts of Page Three driven out of his mind by the worry of discovery.

Smiffy was not so disturbed. He waited for his boss to leave the office on his morning inspection of the animal enclosures, then he fished the newspaper out of the bin and smoothed the wrinkles out of the topless model. Five minutes later his gaze slipped from the nude female and wandered over the rest of the page. A familiar name caught his eye.

'Professor Enrico Steinn, the Nobel Prize winning biologist, died yesterday at his home in Florence, from a massive heart attack. The professor was a firm believer in cryogenics. His body was lowered to a subzero temperature immediately after his death to preserve it ...'

"Steinn? The world is full of Steinns. All of them rich and brainy. That's where I went wrong. Being born a 'Smith.' Maybe I could change my name by deed pole."

Smiffy grumbled at the iniquities of the world, made another mug of tea and promptly forgot about the newspaper report on Professor Steinn's death. He only remembered it when a special delivery of new research equipment arrived at the plant, that same afternoon.

When Smiffy returned from his dinner he found a large wooden crate standing in building 37. 'Boston Cryogenic Company. Handle with care. This way up.' was stencilled on each side of it.

"Cryowhatsit? What the hell has Dr Steinn ordered now? And why put it in unit 37? We don't deal with research equipment. We have enough to do looking after the special livestock projects." Armstrong complained bitterly when he saw the delivery.

"It's cryogenics. The study of preserving dead people at sub zero temperatures." Smiffy recited knowledgeably.

Armstrong peered at his underling through eyes slitted with suspicion. "You been going to that night school again? Been watching University Challenge instead of the football, have you? How come you know more about this than I do?"

"You should read your newspaper properly, and not just peer at the naughty bits." Smiffy retrieved the crumpled Sun from the waste bin, peeled off a soggy tea bag or two and waved the article about Professor Steinn in front of the head keeper's nose.

Armstrong put on his reading glasses and read right through the article before he commented.

"He's a relation, you know."

"Who? To you? Never! Must be on your mother's side."

"No, you bloody twerp! He's related to our Dr Steinn. A cousin or something. They're a brainy lot, these Steinns."

Smiffy looked again at the report on the professor's death and shrugged his shoulders. "Ain't done him much good, has it."

Later in the day, Dr Steinn arrived with several of the security staff and unpacked the new equipment. Armstrong and Smiffy kept well out of the way. They busied themselves cleaning up the animal cages and changing the drinking water, but made sure they kept a close eye on the progress of the unpacking.

"Looks just like a giant metal beer cask to me." Smiffy commented.

"It's a large steel cylinder. All these cryogenic machines look the same." Armstrong tried to sound knowledgeable. He needed to re-establish his superiority.

"Will they fill it with best bitter? Is that how they pickle bodies?"

The head keeper ignored his underling.

Finally the research team filled the metallic tank with liquid nitrogen. Some of the gas spilled out into block 37 like the mist over the moors in a horror film.

"Ooh er! It's just like 'The Hound of the Baskervilles' at the pictures. If Dr Steinn put on a cloak and deerstalker hat, he'd look just like Sherlock Holmes." Smiffy exclaimed in a hoarse whisper.

"Shut up! If he hears you, we're in it up to our necks."

At that precise moment, Dr Steinn did notice the two keepers skulking in a corner. He crooked his finger and beckoned them over to him.

Armstrong hissed out of the corner of his mouth. "I am warning you, Smiffy. Keep your trap shut tight!"

When the two keepers had joined him, Dr Steinn explained briskly. "We are expecting an urgent delivery from Florence. A distant relative of mine is being flown in specially. I want you both here early, to help me make him welcome."

"I don't like it!" Smiffy groaned when the doctor and the security staff had left and he and Armstrong were alone. "First I read about cryogenics in your paper, and all that stuff about a dead professor in Florence, being frozen. Then Doctor Steinn announces a relation of his is coming here from Florence, and we are suddenly overrun with cryogenic paraphernalia. Two and two always make four in my books; mark my words. I'm a trained zoo under-keeper, not a bloody mortician!"

Chapter Eleven

The Duck and Dumplings public house always took a daily newspaper. It was supposedly for the benefit of the customers. When Paddy had read the print off the racing pages he left it on the bar top for the regulars to read.

Tony Tompkins called in for a swift pint on his way home from work. He had drawn the short straw and had supervised detentions, so he was dying for a drink and some peace and quiet. Being the only customer in the bar at that early hour of the evening, he picked up the copy of the pub's newspaper and retreated to a corner table to catch up with the news and to unwind.

An article on silicone enhanced, female lifeguards, grabbed his attention immediately. The bare breasted, blonde model reminded him of Diana Scullery. Not that he had ever seen Diana in the nude, but it was exactly as he had imagined her, on countless occasions. He was so preoccupied with his vision of his new lodger coming out of his bathroom and stripping off her dressing gown in full view of the spy hole, that he missed the article on Professor

Steinn's death. As he flicked through the pages heading for the sports section, he chanced on the centre spread about the strange mythical beast from the fens.

"Good God! Uncle Albert!" Tony forgot himself and exclaimed aloud.

"Where? I didn't hear anyone come in." Paddy shot up from behind the counter and stared at the door.

"Sorry, Paddy. I must have been mistaken," the teacher apologised lamely.

Paddy carried on filling up the bottled beers, but he kept glancing at the lone drinker. He'd heard that hard drugs were changing hands behind the Runford School bicycle sheds, but it had never crossed his mind some of the teachers might be on the stuff as well. Perhaps Tony shared this habit with that weird uncle of his. That would explain some of the strange goings on of late.

Tony stole the centre page of the paper, folded it up small and secreted it in his jacket pocket. Uncle Albert must see this article. The highly touched up photograph accompanying the report was an enlargement of the very Polaroid print his uncle had taken. At first, it crossed his mind that Albert may have contacted the press, but it seemed unlikely as the old fellow shunned publicity, wanting no one to know about his exploits. Pretending to check the football results, Tony read the article under cover of the table. The more he read of it the more he realised it was wildly untrue. If Albert had supplied the information, there would be no talk of devil worship. Nowhere in the article was there any mention of druids, nor of sacrificing a rabbit, and the information was attributed to an 'informed source,' a sure sign that most of it had been invented.

When Tony called to show him the article, Albert was livid.

"I'll murder that bloody Archdruid! What was his name? French Letter? Johnny? Condom? Modnoc the priest! No wonder he wanted a better picture of my Gryphon. No wonder he asked to see the sacrificial site. The man's a fifth columnist, he's a damn spy for the newspapers!"

"I see." Tony said stupidly, because he actually didn't see at all. "Well, you obviously know something about this article. And you don't seem at all pleased with it."

"Too bloody right, boy! Correct on both counts."

"Well, you know what they say, uncle. Don't shoot me, I'm only the messenger. I know you never read the Sun, so when I stumbled across this photo in the pub's newspaper, I tore it out to show you. I hope I did the right thing."

"I suppose I would have found out sooner or later, but I'm glad it was you who told me, Tony. Better to come from you than some snooping reporter after a sensational story, or one of them snide lot in the bar of the Duck and Dumplings. I intend to get even with that sneaky bastard. Archdruid or not, I'll get him. Tell me, are you free to drive your Uncle to Macclesfield this weekend?"

"Where? Macclesfield! Macclesfield in Cheshire? Good grief!"

"I know it's a long way, but I'll pay your petrol and we can set off early. Just don't mention it to your mother, that's all I ask."

Tony knew he couldn't refuse the old chap. He wished, in some ways he'd never opened the newspaper, but wishing would change nothing. He also wished he'd remembered earlier to warn Albert about his mother's plans to marry the old fellow off to one of her WI friends, but Tony decided to keep that bad news to himself. He figured Albert had enough problems on his mind for one day.

Chapter Twelve

Macclesfield in Cheshire is a long way from the Lincolnshire fens. Tony picked up his uncle at the crack of dawn on the Sunday morning and set off up north in the Sierra. By mid morning they were high up in the Peak District, riding the switchback of winding roads through Buxton, the highest town in England, towards their destination. At last, weary but pleased, they drove into Macclesfield itself.

"Coronation Close, you say? Perhaps we'd better ask that fellow on the corner."

Tony wound down his window and checked the route. Coronation Close was a cul-de-sac of nice semi-detached houses, built in the 1950's. He found it easily.

"Well, we're here. Now what?"

Albert didn't stop to answer. Setting his jaw in a determined line, he jumped out of the car.

"Hang on! I'll come with you. I don't want you arrested for inflicting grievous bodily harm!"

They marched up the gravelled path between neatly manicured squares of lawn to the glazed front door, and hesitated on the step of number 21.

Tony tried to peer through the stained glass picture of swallows swooping on a thatched cottage, and into the darkness of the hallway beyond. The chintz curtains and potted plants, visible in the gloom, did not exactly fit his expectations of an Archdruid's palace. He stepped back onto the pebbled path and shook his head in disbelief. But he was secretly relieved that they appeared to be at the wrong house.

"You are sure this is it? Perhaps we'd better go."

"Yes. Look here on the prospectus. 21 Coronation Close. Clear as day."

Tony stared back into the porch, looking for any small clue to confirm that they were in the right place, or better still, to prove they were not.

"Look there! 'Registered Office of the Druids of the Mystic Mistletoe Co Ltd'." Albert pointed smugly at a tiny brass plaque screwed to the brickwork in the darkest recess of the porch. "Now we'll see what the bloody Archdruid has to say for himself."

Tony reached out and pressed the doorbell, then stepped back out of the way. Albert drew himself up to his full five feet two inches, placed his hands on his hips and stood squarely in front of the door, waiting for Modnoc.

A female voice from within shouted. "Someone at the door, dear. Can you get it, I'm just putting the roast in the oven."

The visitors exchanged concerned glances. Could there be an Archdruidess? Albert shrank visibly; he never was very good with the ladies. Tony noticed the reaction and remembered his mother's threat to marry her brother off to some WI widow. Poor Albert, he wouldn't stand a chance. It was like taking a toddler his jabs; by the time he realised what they were doing to him and burst out crying, it would all be over! A key scraped in the lock. The knob turned and the door opened wide.

"Yes? What can I do for you?" Modnoc spoke before he looked properly at his visitors.

"For a start you can explain how my Polaroid picture got in the bloody newspaper!"

Modnoc stared in disbelief at his acolyte and tried to slam the door shut. But Albert was too fast for him and wedged his boot into the doorway.

It was only a brief struggle and it ended abruptly when Mrs Modnoc's voice called from the kitchen. "Ask our visitors to come in, dear." Her husband lost all his fight the instant he heard his partner's voice. He deflated, like a punctured airbag and let go of the doorknob.

"Yes, dear," he muttered meekly, stepping aside to let them enter. Addressing them, he said. "You'd better come through,"

"She's the boss, obviously." Albert whispered in Tony's ear. "I'm certainly glad I never married."

Tony nodded glum agreement.

"Come through to my study." Modnoc ushered his visitors along the hall, past the kitchen with its delicious smell of traditional Sunday lunch, and into a small side room with a window overlooking a tiny back lawn bordered with neatly regimented annual flowers.

"Sit down, Pollawsdoc ... and you young man."

Tony sat beside his uncle on a low leather settee and gazed around the room. His gaze took in the dark oak furniture and the flock wallpaper, punctuated by the occasional black and white photograph, which reminded him of old school photos. There was a wedding group, a line up of policemen and women, looking like the passing out parade at Police College, and a group of serious faced, bowler hatted men, reminding Tony of a group of Freemasons or bank employees. His eyes drifted back to their host, who sat down at his desk, smiling half-heartedly, his arms folded defensively across his chest. Tony relaxed back into the settee and left his uncle to do the talking. He was feeling tired from the early start they had made and the long distance he had driven.

To keep himself from nodding off to sleep, Tony let his eyes wander over the bookshelves, idly reading the titles and trying to guess what sort of a man this Archdruid really was. The teacher reckoned you could tell a lot from a man's reading matter. Soldiers read accounts of military campaigns, athletes read keep-fit manuals and historians studied facsimiles of the Magna Carta and the Domesday Book. Mind you, he thought to himself, I personally prefer girlie magazines. Perhaps I'm an exception to that historian rule, or maybe I've missed my real vocation? He was surprised to see Modnoc's books consisted entirely of accountancy manuals and gardening books. There were at least four volumes on book keeping and several on growing prize carnations. There wasn't a single title about Druidism or any other religion.

Tony glanced out of the window as he tried to make sense of the Archdruid's lack of reading material on his own calling. Suddenly a bright light flashed in his eyes! The sun was reflecting on a mirror in the upstairs window of the house opposite. He frowned and was about to look more closely at the distraction when his attention was drawn back to Modnoc's study.

"...No! I will not agree the Polaroid is your copyright!" Albert was shouting.

Tony was shaken out of his daydreams by the sudden rise in the volume of Uncle Albert's voice. "Why the hell should you have any rights in the beast? I raised It was on my land in the fens. It appeared to me, in my private woods. As far as I can see, you were trespassing anyway!"

"I was not a trespasser. I was there at your invitation, Pollawsdoc, as your superior cleric."

At the thought of being classed as inferior in any way, to the Macclesfield primate, Albert really lost his rag. He shot up from the settee, leaned across the desk and made a grab for Modnoc's throat. Tony pulled him back by his coat tail and tried to calm the old man down. Finally Albert gave in to his nephew's persuasion and sat down again, but he couldn't resist one last taunt.

"If you're so bloody superior, why don't you raise a dragon or something for yourself?"

At that precise moment the door opened and Mrs Modnoc swept in. She had heard the raised voices from the kitchen and rushed to investigate. Perfect timing, Tony thought. Mention a dragon and here indeed was a real live dragon! She was a matronly lady, squat and wide, solidly built, like a brick privy or a Cumberland wrestler. Her sleeves, rolled up to her elbows to facilitate the preparation of Sunday lunch, encompassed a pair of muscular forearms that would not have disgraced a Russian shot-put champion.

"Tut, tut!" She wagged a finger at her husband, who shrank behind his desk like a frightened tortoise retreating into its shell. "That's no way to treat guests, Cuthbert." She scolded him in a broad northern accent. Before Tony had time to curl his lip in a glimmer of a grin at learning Modnoc's real name, the lady of the house turned and beamed at him. "You must be hungry after your journey; t' fens are a long way away. I'm sure you'll not refuse to eat wi' us."

Any lingering doubts Tony had, were overridden by the delicious smell of cooking that had drifted from the kitchen.

"We'd love to, wouldn't we Uncle." He dug Albert sharply in the ribs and accepted for both of them. He was sure after a civilised lunch things could be sorted our amicably. Anyway, breakfast was a distant memory and he was feeling very hungry.

"That's settled then. Give our guests a sherry, Cuthbert. Where's your manners." Like a diplomat who had just settled a difficult dispute at the United Nations, she swept victoriously back to her kitchen.

Lunch was a silent affair. Cuthbert kept his eyes down on his plate as if his meat and two veg were a novel and fascinating experience. Albert ate slowly, glancing sourly at the Archdruid between every mouthful.

"That was a lovely lunch, Mrs Modnoc." Tony tried to lighten the proceedings by praising the cook.

"Do call me Vera," she insisted.

"That lunch was just like my mother makes." Tony ladled on the praise.

"Shall we all go into the lounge?" Vera beamed. "You can open that good sherry we were given last Christmas," she ordered Cuthbert.

Once seated in the lounge under a tasteless brick arch with plaster ducks flying over them, Tony sipped his schooner and waited for the inevitable confrontation.

"I think we are civilised people, Albert. I hope you don't mind me calling you Albert? " Vera gushed. "I am a partner in my husband's little venture with the Druidism; although I'm usually a silent partner."

Modnoc shifted his weight and rolled his eyes in disbelief, but he didn't utter a word. Tony read the telltale signs and grinned to himself. Silent partner, as in the one who pulled the strings, he guessed.

"My husband has every right to use your discovery; it's written into the legal contract.

"Like hell!" Albert started to protest.

Vera held up a silencing finger and shot him a glance that would have stopped the tide. "Let me finish. I know my law; I made sergeant in the Greater Manchester police force before I retired. But, we are civilised folk. Surely we can discuss this amicably and decide on a compromise to suit us all?"

Albert looked doubtful but stayed silent. Tony eyed the lady up and down. She reminded him more and more of his mother. And everybody knew Freda Tompkin's idea of compromise was usually, 'do as I say, or suffer the consequences!' He decided to have his say.

"It's the way your husband publicised this in the national newspapers. My uncle does not want every Fleet Street hack trudging over his private nature reserve, spoiling the countryside and disturbing the wild life. Surely you can see his point of view?"

Vera glared at her husband. "Well? What have you got to say about that?"

"I maybe made a mistake selling…giving that photograph to a press agency. I was naive. I assumed it would go into a nature publication or something more select. I should have insisted where it was used"

"Like hell you did! You went for the maximum return." Albert accused.

"Now, now. You have no proof of that. Anyway, the damage is now done. The Press Agency farm out news to whatever outlets they please. Once we've sold … given the information to them, it's out of our control."

"What a bloody get out!" Albert fumed. "I will see my solicitor in the morning. I will sue you. We'll see if you can wriggle out of it so easily."

Modnoc choked on his sherry. Vera went very pink. They realised Albert was deadly serious in his intentions and with his talk of owning woodland, he probably had the money to go ahead with his threat.

"What about that free Chanting Course?" Modnoc suggested feebly.

"What about a share of the Press fee?" Vera offered, more realistically.

"I don't want your damn money! I want my privacy and that photograph returned. And I want a written undertaking you will not publicise this ever again."

Tony nodded agreement. Uncle Albert was being reasonable, in the circumstances. They couldn't close the stable door after the Gryphon had bolted, so to speak, but they could rule out further trouble.

"We can do that, can't we Cuthbert?"

The Archdruid squirmed in his chair. "I do not have the polaroid. I sold it to the agency."

"Well you either get it back or I'll sue." Albert put down his untouched sherry and rose to leave. Those were his last words on the subject and he saw no reason to talk any more. "Come on nephew. We have a long journey home." Turning to the

Archdruid, he hissed. "I'll give you one week. If that picture's not back in my possession by next Saturday, I'll go straight to my solicitor."

Chapter Thirteen

Albert stomped down the path from Modnoc's front door, without a backward glance. He stood impatiently at the side of the Sierra, stamping his boots to remove all traces of the place and fuming with frustration while he waited for his nephew to catch up with him.

Tony thanked Vera for the lunch and followed his uncle to the car. As he walked down the path, his eyes were dazzled again by the same bright light that shone from the window across the road. He assumed the sun was reflecting on a mirror or some glass object straight into his eyes. Stopping at the gate, he put a hand up to shield his eyes and looked directly up at the bedroom window. He was just in time to notice a small figure jump furtively back from the window and dissolve into the shadows of the room. Tony shielded his eyes with both hands and stared intently at the window. With a shock he realised the sun's rays had been reflecting off the lens of a brass telescope, which was still clearly visible on its tripod, with the object lens pressed up against the window. Tony stopped in his tracks. He made a deliberate point of looking up towards the window to scowl at the Peeping Tom and register his disapproval.

"Come on. We've no reason to hang about here," Albert said, exasperation showing in his voice. He was dying to be setting off for Runford.

Tony had other things on his mind. He was annoyed and a little intrigued at being spied on. It was OK for him to plan to spy on his lodger, but it was another ball game when he was the target.

"Don't look now, Uncle, but someone has been spying on us through a telescope, from the house opposite."

Albert swung around and looked at the row of houses.

"I'm not surprised. I bet all this neighbourhood is full of crooks! Just like that lame excuse for an Archdruid!"

Tony grinned to himself. Modnoc had certainly rubbed Albert up the wrong way. He searched in his pocket for the car keys and grasped the handle of the driver's door.

"Oi! You there. Pst!" A gravelly voiced hissed.

It took Tony several seconds to realise the comments were aimed at them. He looked over his shoulder, curious to know who could want them. After all, he and his uncle were strangers to Macclesfield, and had no other business there.

Albert ignored the interruption. He was too engrossed in his own thoughts of revenge. He muttered darkly to himself. "I'll ring my solicitor the minute we get in and ask his advice."

"Pst! You there." The call was repeated.

Tony turned to see who was trying to attract their attention. He spotted a scrawny old man, hiding behind the gatepost of the house across the road. The newcomer was so thin the gatepost did indeed almost hide him. When he stepped from behind the post, Tony took a good look at him. The man was small with lank grey hair flopped down over his forehead. His bony hands were clasped together like a praying mantis. He looked seedy and unwashed from the top of his greasy hair to his grubby oversized bedroom slippers.

"Are you calling us?" Tony asked, hoping it was some mistake.

"Pollawsdoc, isn't it? I thought it must be you."

At this use of his name, Albert stood upright and turned to face the old man. "Who are you? How do you know my druid name?"

"I know your name because I christened you...in a manner of speaking. You see, I'm the original Archdruid of Macclesfield."

Albert frowned in disbelief. Tony's mouth dropped open. If this was the original Archdruid, what was Modnoc? Where exactly did the bowler hatted businessman and this poor old fellow fit into the grand cosmic scheme of things?

"Follow me." The thin, bent figure ran quickly up the pathway of the house like a startled grey squirrel, and vanished around the back way.

Tony turned to look at his uncle for guidance. He hesitated and raised an enquiring eyebrow, hoping they could ignore the invitation and start for home, but Albert was already halfway across the road. This new development was far too intriguing for him to miss.

When they had followed the old chap into his house and caught up with him, he cleared a space on a lumpy settee and smiled a toothless smile at them. "Sit yourself down. I will introduce myself properly. I am Enoesiw, the Archdruid of Macclesfield. I'm the chief druid in the land, trained from my early teens to assume the awesome mantle of head of the old religion."

"What about him over the road?" Tony snorted. "I knew he wasn't genuine. Is he an impostor or something?"

"Well not exactly." The old man conceded.

Albert nodded as if he was beginning to understand.

"My first lesson spoke of the Wise One. That's you isn't it. Enoesiw spelled backwards is Wise One."

Tony rolled his eyes in disbelief and sought guidance from above by staring at the ceiling. Unfortunately the yellowed cracked plaster gave him no help whatsoever. Yet another ridiculous name spelled backwards, he groaned inwardly, but out loud he asked. "Then, how come that twit across the road has taken over? He says he bought the religion from you, as if it was a business."

"It's a long story."

"I bet it is! How could he have bought the business from the previous Archdruid? Do explain." Tony persisted.

Enoesiw looked sheepishly down at his oversized bedroom slippers. "He did indeed buy the title from me. I hit on hard times when my wife was ill and I sold him the rights to the name and the acolytes basic training manual." The old man spread his hands in a gesture of helplessness. "I have regretted it ever since, but I badly needed the money. My health was failing and she was dying. There was no one of the right calibre to succeed me. I have hundreds of faithful followers but none of them had the call." His voice fell almost to a whisper and his chest rose and fell as if he would sob.

Albert patted the old chap reassuringly on his thin shoulders. "I just knew that twit couldn't be a real Archdruid. He didn't have a clue how I conjured up that mythical beast."

"Ah! The mythical beast! It's true then? I heard rumours. One of my old followers sent me a copy of a newspaper with a blurred photograph of a Gryphon in it. I found out my neighbour had sold the original picture to the press. I've kept the house under surveillance trying to find out more. I knew he couldn't have done it himself. He hasn't the imagination for it."

"That telescope!" Tony interrupted. "You were spying on us all the time, through a telescope!"

"I had to know who had the power to do such a thing. The druid who could conjure up a Gryphon should by rights be my true successor. Power like that is not granted to many." He turned to face Albert "That is, if I can believe you really materialised a Gryphon?"

"I did it twice. I haven't been able to repeat it."

The Wise One frowned. "Tell me which ceremony you used. Perhaps I can give you a reason for that."

"I used the one at the end of lesson two. The ceremony that uses a sacrificial rabbit."

The old Archdruid's frown deepened and he nervously stroked the stubble on his chin.

"Is that a problem?" Albert could see there were doubts.

`"No; not exactly. That ceremony is intended as a thanksgiving for the fruits of the earth. Not to raise power at all."

"I know." It was Albert's turn to look puzzled. "I was performing it to give thanks for my woods when the beast turned up. Does that matter?"

"No, Pollawsdoc. What matters, is that you raised the Gryphon. Nothing else is important. But I can't think how you did it, for the life of me."

Tony shook his head and smiled a sneaky kind of grin.

Albert turned angrily on his nephew. "What? Don't just sit there grinning, boy. Come out with it!"

"I was only thinking to myself how you raised this Gryphon, but when Di and I were present nothing happened."

"So? Are you accusing me of something?" Albert turned red with anger.

"No, uncle. I was just voicing my thoughts. You know I've been sceptical from the very first."

The Wise One hurriedly stepped in as peacemaker. "You are right to be sceptical, young man. We cannot accept anyone's word as proof positive. But there is the photograph. Do you think it's a fake?"

"No." Tony spread his hands in a gesture of helplessness. "I can't see how it can be a fake. Anyway, my Uncle Albert is so honest you could trust him with your life."

"Good." The Wise One nodded his agreement. "I count myself as a good judge of character and that is how I felt about Pollawsdoc, the minute I met him. Which leaves only one interpretation of his results. He raised a Gryphon by some means or other, which we, I include myself in that, which we can't understand."

Albert wasn't completely mollified by this statement. He protested "Young Diana is a biologist and she believed me."

Tony shook his head but said nothing. He thought, I don't understand her attitude either. I'm not even convinced she's being straight with either of us about that Gryphon. But out loud he said. "I agree."

"There you are then. I believe in you enough to start your training and to let my followers know I have found my true successor." The Wise One smiled reassuringly and put his bony arm around Albert's shoulders.

Albert took a step back and shook his head. He enjoyed studying religions but did he want to be responsible for hundreds of followers? He was a loner, used to paddling his own canoe and answering to nobody. This was not what he wanted at all.

The old Archdruid noticed Albert's hesitation, but completely misread his reasons. He grabbed Albert's hand and hung on to it desperately.

"Don't worry about your lack of knowledge. I will teach you all I know, just as my mentor taught me. You'll have no difficulty understanding the rituals. You've surpassed my meagre achievements already."

Albert looked at the upturned face and noticed the tears welling up in the old man's eyes. He held onto the scrawny hand and patted it gently. "I'm not worthy."

"That just shows how suitable you are. True humility is rare."

Tony looked on open mouthed at this exchange. Uncle Albert, successor to the Archdruid? His mother would never accept it. The regulars at the pub wouldn't dare swear in his presence. What would the tourist board make of it? Maybe I'll have to call him Your Holiness or something equally stupid. His mind boggled at the possible repercussions.

Albert was having doubts of another kind. "I've made a wide study of world religions. Covered most of them by now. How come I've never heard of you, if you have so many followers?"

"We druids are a secretive lot. Anyway my druid name is known to very few."

"What's your real name then?" Albert persisted, growing suspicious at this reluctance to divulge information.

The old druid sighed deeply. He could see Albert was not going to be fobbed off with excuses, and he had to admit, he had a point.

"William Arthur Cobbold. That's my real name, as you call it."

"Not THE William Arthur Cobbold?"

Tony raised his eyebrows. Who the hell was this man? Albert had obviously seen or heard the name before and was impressed, but it meant absolutely nothing to him.

"Are you really the William Arthur Cobbold who levitated in front of the world's press and had his photograph on the front of Wisdom Today?"

The Archdruid looked down sheepishly at his feet and nodded silent agreement.

Albert had been thinking feverishly, trying to recall the newspaper reports from all those years ago. It was in the late 1970's, he remembered. Most of the popular press carried a photograph of this poor man on a stretcher, swathed in bandages, and in obvious pain. The injuries appeared to be to his legs and feet. Albert glanced down at the old druid's size fourteen slippers. It all fell into place then. He remembered how the casualty in the press photographs had these huge bandaged feet sticking up from the end of the stretcher. At the time he thought it was all surgical dressings, but now he realised the man just had a pair of huge feet beneath a thin layer of bandages.

"There was something of a mystery about that levitation; if I recall rightly. Every newspaper carried a report that you had tried to levitate but had fallen from the top of a block of flats and broken both your legs. That was the story in every newspaper but one. 'Wisdom Today' reported that you did actually fly up from the ground but then you accidentally fell and injured yourself. If I remember rightly, they had a photograph of you floating several feet above the ground. What really did happen that day? Did you really manage to levitate?"

"I did. And I fell. It's the old Adam and Eve story. Woman caused Man to fall from grace and he was banned from the Garden of Eden."

Tony coughed aloud at this moral from the scriptures. True Archdruid or not, this little runt obviously took himself very seriously.

"I meditated on weightlessness and rose twenty feet up into the air; the highest I'd ever managed. Wisdom's photographer was the only one there at the time. The other reporters were late and arrived just as I fell down to earth again."

"How come you fell? Anything to do with Saint Michael and the devil?" Tony enquired sarcastically, choosing as unlikely a religious analogy as he could invent.

"In a way, yes. it was indeed the devil and his tempting. I hovered at twenty feet and was full of my own importance. Foolishly, I decided to go higher. I rose another ten feet, which brought me level with the top windows of the flats. That was my undoing. I was younger then, you understand." Enoesiw took out a blue spotted handkerchief and loudly blew his nose.

"And then? Go on man, don't leave us in the air along with you, so to speak." Albert prompted.

"It was the old Adam that was my undoing. Mavis Harbottle, the usherette from the Roxy, lived in that top floor flat. She was just getting dressed with her curtains open. I suppose she never dreamed she be overlooked at that height. By gum! She was a well built lass. The sight of her bare double D's put levitation completely out of my mind. I lost it and I fell. The rest of the story, you and the world knows about."

"But you did fly!" Albert eyes gleamed with the knowledge of the old man's triumph.

"Aye lad. I did fly. But I've never had the nerve to fly so high again."

"Is that when you developed such big feet?" Tony asked, trying hard not to laugh at the whole incredible story. He knew it was all too ridiculous for words, but secretly he was beginning to warm to the old chap. He himself would have been proud of that escapade with the big-breasted girl.

"No, lad. I've always had huge feet; even when I was a little nipper. That's the main reason I rose rapidly through the ranks of the Northern Druids in the first place. Big feet give you a great advantage at Clogarte."

Tony frowned. Clogarte? Whatever that meant! He didn't bother to pursue the question. It was all becoming too laughable and he had heard quite enough tall stories for one day. First there was the Mythical Gryphon now this little old pensioner claimed he could fly! He didn't voice his doubts because Albert seemed thrilled with what he'd found out. But then, his uncle was a bit of a fanatic about religions.

"Eventually I'd like you to take over from me, Pollawsdoc. You don't have to make your mind up right now. I'm probably good for another six months before I go to that great stone circle in the sky. Let me give you private lessons to prepare you for the role.

When you think you are ready we will discuss it again," the old Archdruid pressed.

"But I'm from the Lincolnshire fens. It's miles down south and I can't keep travelling all this way up north to Macclesfield."

"I have much of the knowledge written out. I expected to die before I found a suitable candidate so I've committed most of the important mysteries to paper. I've prepared a set of study tapes based on self-hypnotic principles, and once you have mastered the thought transference system, we can communicate by thought alone. Distance will be no problem."

Albert's face lit up again. The possibility of mind reading and of thought transference fascinated him. The chance of actually levitating held his imagination enthralled. Anything esoteric interested him. "Well maybe I could try a few lessons from you and see how I get on."

The old druid's face creased in a big smile. He leaned on Albert's arm, patted his hands and nodded his head in satisfaction.

Tony shook his head, tutted under his breath and frowned deeply. All this talk of mind reading, of self-hypnosis, of levitation, and of hundreds of fanatical followers, worried him. Uncle Albert was getting in too deep. It was one thing playing at being a Buddhist monk but this was a different kettle of fish altogether He'd be in over his head before he knew it.

"We shall soon have to go, Uncle. It's a long way home." Tony tried to change the subject and hurry them away.

"The impatience of youth." Enoesiw said warmly. "I will get the lessons and the tapes. You can take them with you."

Albert nodded happily. Here was a chance to really learn about a new religion at the feet of a master. Reverently, he took the sheaf of hand written notes and the audio cassettes, and folded them into his pocket.

"I'll look after them. Can I contact you in a more convenient way if I get any queries?"

The old man wrote a phone number on a piece of paper. "I don't have a telephone, but that number will get a message to me. He's a loyal follower of mine with a mobile phone."

Tony and Albert left the old Archdruid at his gate.

"Never fear, Wise One, I'll be in touch." Albert assured him.

"I will let my followers know I have found the new, true, trainee Archdruid."

Albert looked startled at this remark but he hadn't the heart to contradict the old man when he saw the far away look in his tired eyes and the obvious happiness on his lined face.

As they motored homewards, Tony raised the subject of Clogarte with his uncle.

"Well! That was a turn up for the books. I suppose you knew what the old fellow was on about when he said his big feet were useful for Clogarte?"

"No, Tony. I hadn't a clue. But no doubt these lessons will reveal all, in good time." He gave a self-satisfied grin and patted the bulge in his coat pocket.

Tony scowled to himself and concentrated on his driving.

Chapter Fourteen

Neither of the Steinn brothers read the Sun and no one chose to tell them there was a report of a Gryphon loose in the fens. Certainly their animal keepers kept very quiet about the embarrassing story. The rumour of their hybrids excursions into Albert's woods would have passed the brothers by, but for Frank Steinn's young nephew.

Frank spent the weekend with his sister at her home. Over coffee he flicked through the Sunday Times, checking the share index for the major pharmaceutical companies and his competitors, then he threw the broadsheet aside to play with his nephew. Young Sidney always asked his uncle to read to him from his latest collection of comics. 'Adventures for Boys' was his first choice.   Uncle Frank read aloud the latest episode in the life of Barry, the teenage astronaut, then turned to his own favourite column, The Wonders of Modern Science. This section usually showed cutaway diagrams of racing cars, space shuttles, and the like, but that month the regular column had been replaced by one with a natural history flavour.

'Fabulous Beasts of Antiquity,' the headline read. The Sphinx of early Egypt, the Dragons of old England, the Centaurs of ancient Greece, were all mentioned. This subject fascinated Frank Steinn because he felt he was involved in recreating some of these myths. Suddenly his attention was arrested by a reference to a modern day Gryphon, reputed to roam the fens of South Lincolnshire. Special report and photograph on page seven, the copy read. Frank slammed down his coffee cup and rifled frantically through the pages of the comic. When he found the page his eyes bulged out of his head. "Hells Bells! I can't believe it! It's my Eagle-dog!" He slammed his fist on the table sending his empty cup up into the air and onto the carpet. Frank really lost his temper before he noticed the horror in the child's eyes at this violent outburst. Sidney screamed out loud. Frank's sister ran in from the kitchen.

"Is everything alright?" She grabbed the boy up from the floor and hugged him to her breast, pressing one of his ears against her body and covering the other with a soothing hand.

"Sorry, sis. I just realised we have pressing problems at the Runford site."

"I do wish you'd leave your business problems at work. You frightened Sidney to death."

"Hell bells! He did." Sidney mimicked.

Dr Steinn could hardly wait to get back to the Runford plant.

On Monday morning Dr Frank Steinn arrived unusually early at Runford. He strode into the office before his secretary had even opened the post.

She looked up in surprise at this early visit. "Good morning. Coffee sir?"

"Damn your coffee! Have you seen this report in this magazine?" He held out the crumpled comic in front of her nose.

"I can't say I actually ever read that particular …er… periodical…"

"Well you damn well should! Look here. This is definitely a photograph of one of our secret experiments from building 37."

She took the comic and stared curiously at the highly touched up picture. Few people were allowed near building 37. It was involved in such hush-hush projects, if it was mentioned in the comic, she wanted to see for herself.

"A Gryphon? Are you sure? There's so much airbrush work it could be my neighbour's dog with a chicken perched on its head."

Steinn rose from his seat and stormed towards the door. "I'll go and see that damn incompetent zoo keeper, what's-his -name? Headstrong or something."

"Armstrong, sir."

As soon as he strode out of the office, the secretary rushed to her desk and tried to raise building 37 on the internal telephone. She'd seen the murderous glint in her employer's eyes and she was genuinely worried for Armstrong's safety.

Armstrong got the message and had four minutes to prepare himself for Dr Steinn's arrival. He had dreaded this would happen, since the publication of the original photograph in the daily paper. He had thought of little else and had suffered regular nightmares about it. However, as each successive day had passed with no outburst from his boss, he had breathed more easily, and even kidded himself he was out of trouble. Now the balloon was going up. He reassured himself, at least his nagging fears had given him plenty of time to prepare a defence.

"Smiffy, if anything's said, deny all knowledge of it. Act as if we are as shocked as everybody else. It's a fuzzy picture anyway, so we can pretend we don't believe it's our animal."

When Dr Steinn stormed into the animal rooms, Armstrong was sweeping the floor, whistling nonchalantly to himself.

"What do you know about this?" Steinn held up the offending picture.

Armstrong leaned on his broom. Deliberately, he didn't put it aside in case he should need it to defend himself. Taking his reading glasses slowly from his inside pocket he made a show of reading the comic book.

"Haven't seen this since I was a nipper. Still a good read, is it sir?"

"Look at that photograph. That's our Eagle-dog, isn't it? What have you to say about that?"

Armstrong peered at the damning evidence, pursed his lips doubtfully and rotated the page to look at the picture from every angle, just as he did with the Page Three pin-up girls.

"I don't think so, sir. It could be anything, it's so touched up."

"Don't give me that! You, or your stupid sidekick, have sold this photograph to the press."

Armstrong swallowed hard. It was bad enough that somebody had breached security and photographed the Eagle-dog, but to be unjustly accused of committing the crime himself, that was big trouble. He shouted for Smiffy.

"What do you know about this?" He handed over the comic to his under-keeper, giving him a warning glare.

"Nice." Smiffy smiled vacantly. "Not as good as the photo in the Sun though, is it."

Armstrong choked like a man who had swallowed his own tongue. Dr Steinn glared at the two keepers as if his eyes would shrivel them.

"The Sun? You mean this photograph was in the national newspapers? The world knows what we are doing in building 37? This is a disaster! We'll have government snoopers crawling all over the place."

"Begging your pardon, sir. It doesn't actually mention building 37 or this plant. These reporter fellows obviously don't know where the creature is"

"But the person who took the photograph must know it's here, it stands to reason." Dr Steinn's mind was working overtime. If he could find out where the newspaper bought the photograph, he might be able to silence the source. He would have to bring security onto it.

"Hopefully, that's the last we'll hear of it." Armstrong voiced his own hopes.

"Just give them and the authorities time. Just give them time. They'll nag away at this story like a starving toddler at a teething ring." The doctor had the last word as he left the building on his way to see the security chief.

Chapter Fifteen

"I must say that picture of an alleged Gryphon, could be almost anything, sir. It could be a chicken sitting on a dog's head." The security chief tried to dismiss the problem by belittling the evidence. If there had been a breach of security his neck was on the block.

"Rubbish, Bowls! Not you as well!" Steinn growled. "You know and I know, someone has been in here and photographed that creature. You will do the job I pay you to do. Contact the newspaper to find out where they bought this picture."

Richard Bowls didn't argue. He was delighted to apparently get off so lightly.

The trail of the Polaroid print was easy to follow. The comic book publisher and the newspaper office who had reproduced the picture, were both most helpful.

"This is the Runford Church Magazine. The Reverent Bowls speaking" The chief put on his vicar's voice when he questioned the newspaper office. "I was phoning to ask where we could get permission to reproduce a photograph you used recently."

"Right vicar, was it one on Page Three or the footballers on the back page?" the sub editor asked.

"Actually it was a picture of a Gryphon seen in the fens."

"What the hell do you want that for? Begging your pardon, vicar, no offence meant."

Richard Bowls had to think fast. He found that was the trouble with lying, he always had to invent more lies to cover up.

"We are doing an article on...er the er...the...dangers of dabbling with witchcraft. Yes that's it. It will be a warning to teenagers. Especially as we are in the fens and your article said the incident was in this area."

"Hang on. I'll check which agency sold us the picture." The sub editor left the phone for five minutes then came back with the information. "It was a small northern outfit. The Cheshire News Agency."

The security chief was pleased with his detective work. He left a message to prove to Dr Steinn that he was making progress, then continued with his enquiries.

"Is that the Cheshire News Agency?"

"Yes, What can we do for you?"

"This is the police." Bowls changed his story. He felt much more at home with that one, being an ex-copper. "We have reason to believe you sold to several news outlets, a picture purporting to be of a Gryphon."

"So what?"

Bowls could hear from his tone of voice that the man wasn't easily frightened. He tried a different tack. "We need the picture to mount a ...a... spot the Gryphon competition in the Police Gazette."

"Right. I'll send you the print, if you first send the money."

Bowls felt he would not find the source of the print by just asking. He had sudden inspiration.

"Just one thing. Can you definitely prove this is not a fake photograph? In our position, we couldn't use anything suspect, you understand."

"Well...no. Our photographer didn't take this particular shot. I suppose I could put you on to the man who sold it to us. Hang on a minute, I'll check if that's possible"

Bowls grinned in triumph. He was getting the information without any leg-work.

"Hello. Are you there? We were sold it by as bloke calling himself Modnoc. He gave his address as 21 Coronation Close, Macclesfield. We didn't sign an anonymity clause, so there's no harm in telling you...you being the police, of course."

"Of course."

"Now, how do you intend to pay, and where do we send your copy?"

"Hang on a minute. I'll check the authenticity first, then get back to you." Bowls slammed down the telephone. He had his lead, now to follow it up. This chap Modnoc could be the man who somehow managed to breach their security. He'd have to tread carefully. It would be foolish to phone him and alert him to their enquiries.

A personal visit is the answer. Bowls grinned at the thought. It was years since he had worked in the field for the vice squad. He had always enjoyed putting fear into suspects in the course of his duty.

"Just like the old days. I'll enjoy a day up in Macclesfield at the company's expense," he muttered, then he telephoned Steinn's secretary and left another message, explaining where he was going.

Bowls chose one of his biggest security guards to drive the car and to provide him with some back-up. They set out for the north after their morning coffee break, taking one of the firm's fastest cars.

Modnoc and his wife, Vera, were in the garden when their visitors arrived.

"Someone at the front door, dear." Cuthbert looked up from his planting.

"Well go and answer it." Vera made no move to rise from her deck-chair. She didn't even bother to look up from her newspaper.

Modnoc dutifully wiped his hands on his apron and took the side path to the front door.

"Yes?" He eyed the two burly men suspiciously.

"Mr Modnoc?" Bowls asked.

"Yes, that's me. Who's asking?"

"Police." The security chief flashed his Steinn Brothers security card just long enough to make it look official. "My colleague and I need a private word with you."

"You'd better come round the back." Modnoc led the visitors to the back door.

Vera glanced up from here newspaper and eyed the men suspiciously. She had spent several years in the Greater Manchester police force as a vice squad sergeant. She was so experienced, she could tell plain-clothes police officers at fifty metres. These two didn't seem quite right.

"Two policemen come to have a word with us, dear." Modnoc explained.

"Oh! What about?"

Bowls didn't waste any time on preliminaries. "We have reason to believe you sold this to a photographic agency." He pushed the picture of the Gryphon under Modnoc's nose.

Modnoc blushed and looked most guilty. Several possibilities flitted through his mind, but his main concern was the threat of legal action that Pollawsdoc had promised. He looked at Vera in panic.

Vera rose from her deckchair and folded her arms across her chest. "So what? It's not a crime, is it?"

Bowls shot her a quick glance and realised she would not be intimidated by him. He retreated, stepping behind his large colleague and pushing him to the fore.

Vera smiled disarmingly at them both. "When I worked for the Manchester police, plain clothes officers always carried identification with them. Let's see yours."

"We've already shown it to him." Bowls nodded to her husband.

"Then you won't mind showing it to me, will you."

The second security man took a step forward, prepared for trouble.

Vera dropped her hands to her side and smiled at them again. "I was northern area police judo champ for four years. Just you try me!"

The heavy smiled apologetically. Bowls cringed and decided it would be wise to tell her a slightly altered version of the truth.

"We aren't really police, madam. I just said that to avoid trouble. We are security staff working for the laboratory that owns the Gryphon. The creature is part of a secret government project. Somehow our security must have been compromised to get that photograph."

Modnoc choked. Thoughts of Albert's solicitor paled against upsetting a confidential government project.

Vera turned on her husband in disbelief.

"You stupid man! You went with that silly acolyte of yours to check this out. How come you didn't notice it was at an official government project?"

"It was in some ordinary woods, dear. It was not a research establishment. Honestly!"

Bowls interrupted them. "Beggars Bush Woods, was it, sir?"

"Yes, that's correct."

121

"That's right next to our facilities. Our barbed wire fence runs alongside those woods."

"There you are, Cuthbert. You were fooled by that old chap. What was his name? Pollawsdoc or something similar."

"Ah! So you do recognise the photograph and you can tell us who took it?

"Yes. I'll tell you with pleasure. I never really trusted the chap from the first time he offered me the photograph. It was a man called Albert Williams who lives just up the road from your plant, in Runford."

Bowls sighed with relief. He had a name and an approximate address, and he'd avoided trouble with Vera. He shook hands with Modnoc and thanked him for his help, anxious to be back on the road to Runford. But Vera had other ideas. She stepped behind the two security men, cutting off their retreat to the road.

"I suppose you are going to pay us for this information?" She folded her arms again and flexed her shoulders so that her bulging biceps could be seen rippling under her blouse sleeves.

"Ah! Yes of course. Fancy me forgetting. Will a tenner do?"

She eyed him disdainfully, but said nothing.

"What about twenty?" He held out two crisp ten pound notes.

"When I was in the force, fifty was the usual amount."

Bowls emptied his wallet and reluctantly paid her. He knew he might have trouble trying to convince the boss's secretary he had paid that amount for information, but he had his job and his health to consider.

On the way back to Runford, the security chief wrote a report for Dr Steinn and sealed it in an envelope marked confidential. When they arrived at the plant he handed it to the secretary for the research director's personal attention, then took the rest of the day off.

Next morning Bowls was summoned to the boss' office.

"Good work, Bowls. See my secretary about any incidental expenses. I understand it's our old friend Mr Albert Williams we have to thank for this problem."

"Oh! You know him, sir?"

"Oh yes. He's a bit of a crank. The last time I saw him he was playing at being a Buddhist monk in Runford market place. We bought the land from him when we built this plant. He still owns the woods next door. He wouldn't part with those. I wondered why at the time."

"He probably kept those woods just to spy on us, sir. That explains a lot."

"It doesn't explain how he managed to photograph a creature locked inside building 37.

"Yes, of course, sir. I'm investigating that." Bowls cringed.

"Keep your eyes and ears open, Bowls. Just in case Williams gets up to more funny business, better double the security on that section of the perimeter fence between his woods and our land." Steinn waved his hand at the security chief, dismissing him from the office.

Bowls didn't move.

"Well?" Steinn asked.

"Would you like me to kidnap this Albert Williams chap and bring him into the plant to answer to you, sir?"

"No. Heavens no! He's a well respected man in Runford. He has family there. We'd have the police on us like a ton of bricks. Just keep an eye out for him at the perimeter fence. Maybe we'll consider your suggestion, if he tries any more funny business."

Chapter Sixteen

Albert Williams had been thrilled to get home from Cheshire and make a start on his studies. The thought of learning the secrets of druidism from the real Archdruid of Macclesfield drove him on to make a superhuman effort. He studied every waking hour of every day and hardly slept at all. By the middle of the week he had learned how to induce self-hypnosis, and found he could assimilate knowledge at a phenomenal rate while in a trance. This skill greatly accelerating the learning process.

Albert's drinking cronies missed his regular appearances at the Duck and Dumpling and questions were asked about his state of health.

"Albert alright, is he? Only, we've not seen hair nor hide of him for days." Paddy asked Tony when he dropped in mid week for a drink, on his way home from a late session at school.

"I've no idea. He was OK when I saw him on Sunday. I'll have to call in on him when I can make time." Tony was busy getting the spare bedroom ready for his new lodger. There was the furniture to be bought from the second hand dealers and the bedding and linen to be obtained. He also had to make sure every stick of furniture was placed correctly to ensure he would see a lot of his new lodger. A lot more than she would have wanted!

Tony decided he had better call on his uncle that very evening. He rang the doorbell several times and even went to the back door and knocked loudly on it, before he managed to attract the old chap's attention.

"You alright, Albert? They were asking after you at the pub."

"Come in, lad, and shut the door. I'm fine. I'm just too busy to bother with beer drinking at present."

Tony frowned. 'Too busy to bother with beer drinking?' He could never imagine himself being that busy. This was serious! Tony wondered if the old man was ill. He looked him up and down but he looked a picture of health.

"What's so important then?"

"You know what's so important to me. You were there when I was given the lessons. I've been working hard at my studies and I'm absolutely fascinated by my progress. I've mastered the art of self hypnosis and I can already use the mental telepathy." Albert grinned with satisfaction. "I've managed to contact the Wise One several times but the signal keeps breaking up like the reception on the crystal radio I made as a boy. Still, we have communicated a little."

"On the mobile phone you mean?"

"Course not, Tony! I mean by thought transference, by mental telepathy!"

Tony grunted in disbelief and thought, 'whatever next will the old devil kid himself he can do?'

"I'll tell you whatever next the old devil will kid himself he can do." Albert repeated aloud Tony's thoughts.

Tony's mouth fell open. "How did you do that?"

"If you'd listened to me you'd have heard me say I am perfecting my mental telepathy skills." Albert grinned in triumph. "I must say I had more success with you than I'm having with the Wise One. Maybe it's because I can actually see your face? Maybe its because the thoughts don't have so far to travel? What do you think?"

Tony was too startled to answer aloud but he shook his head and thought, whatever next?

"Whatever next? For your information, the very next thing I want to do is learn to levitate. Once I've found out how to make good contact with the Wise One by telepathy, I'll ask him to teach me to fly. "

Tony swallowed hard. He could not believe the evidence of his own ears. "Do that again, Uncle Albert. Read my mind again."

"OK. Try thinking of what you were hoping to do when you get home."

Tony grinned to himself as he remembered his little scheme to see more of Di when she moved in.

"Oh naughty!" Albert exclaimed. "It won't work though. She's too bright not to notice the lens."

Tony choked and went bright red with embarrassment. He tried to cover up his confusion.

"Uncle! I don't know what you mean. You've made it all up." He was searching for an excuse to leave before Albert discovered everything he had planned, when there was a loud ring on the front doorbell. He jumped at the chance to get away. "I'll get it, uncle. Then I must go." He rushed to answer the doorbell.

Freda Tompkins, Tony's mother, was standing on the front step when he opened it. She didn't wait to be invited inside, but pushed her way past her son and walked into the kitchen.

"Hello, Freda dear." Albert smiled as if he was pleased to see her. "Come to invite me round to tea, have you?"

Freda frowned. "Yes. As a matter of fact I have."

"Well I wouldn't bother to ask your widow friend from the WI. I am not getting married to her or anyone else!"

Freda sat down heavily on the nearest kitchen chair. She let out her breath like a punctured balloon. All her plans were thwarted. Her brother knew all about her little deception. She considered the position. How the hell had Albert found out about her little plot? Suddenly she thought of the only possible logical answer.

"Tony! Anthony! I want a word with you!"

On his way to the door, Tony had heard the exchange between his mother and her brother. It took no mind reader to know he would get the blame for all this. He was already running up the road before his mother could get up from her chair.

Chapter Seventeen.

The day of the school visit to Steinn Pharmaceutical Plant arrived quickly. Diana Scullery had persuaded ten of her sixth form Biology students to go on the visit, but she was disappointed, because ten was really not enough. She had hoped for twice that number to impress on the staff at the research plant, and to her headmaster, just how committed her students were to the visit.

Rey Muldoon, who had a free morning on that day, put his name down to accompany the group. He decided to raise the profile of the visit by persuading some of his PE students to go as well. He used various methods of coercion to get them to volunteer.

"Dickinson. You have not done PE this term yet. I know you are pulling the old trick of a pebble in your shoe. I've seen you remove it and run out of the school gate as soon as the last bell rings."

Dickinson blushed with guilt and swallowed hard. This could cost him detention for a week at least, or maybe a daily cross country run after school. He toyed with the idea of playing his trump card and telling Mr Muldoon he knew about the teacher's liaison with Miss Scullery behind the bike sheds, but discretion and common sense prevailed. He realised just in time, that Rey Muldoon and Diana Scullery were breaking no school rules by meeting behind the bicycle sheds, but he was, especially when he went for a smoke during lessons!

Muldoon grinned triumphantly at Dickinson's obvious discomfort. "Now, what can you do for me to make amends, eh? I'm sure I can think of an appropriate punishment."

Dickinson closed his eyes, gritted his teeth, and awaited his fate. The man had a cruel streak in him. It would be a hundred press-ups at least.

"You are one of those animal rights protestors, aren't you?" Muldoon sounded almost friendly.

Dickinson opened his eyes wide. That was not what he had been expecting to hear. It confused him. He nodded sullen agreement.

"I thought so." Muldoon punched his fist into his hand and smiled broadly. "As a punishment, you are going to volunteer to go on this school visit to the Steinn Brothers plant with the Biology group."

Dickinson looked aghast at his PE teacher. "That's a diabolical punishment, Sir! You can't make me watch poor helpless animals being butchered for science, Sir! Its inhuman, Sir! Surely it's against the Geneva Convention? I demand one hundred press-ups."

"Who said anything about watching experiments, Dickinson. You could always close your eyes. Anyway, I have a special job for you. I saw you protesting outside the plant. You surely wouldn't want to miss a chance to wave your animal rights banners inside?"

Dickinson swallowed hard and thought even harder. He had never thought of the PE teacher as an animal lover but he had to believe the evidence of his own ears. His face broke into a conspiratorial grin. "I'd love to come on the visit, Sir."

"Good lad. I thought you might. But no word of this to Miss Scullery, you understand. We don't want to worry her, do we."

That last remark really left Dickinson pondering. Mr Muldoon couldn't fancy the Biology teacher or he wouldn't want to spoil her school visit like that. Maybe she'd turned him down? Maybe Mr Tompkins was the flavour of the month after all? What was that quote about a lover scorned? His mother had dropped a remark along those lines as she watched a TV soap the previous evening. Whatever the reason behind it all, he knew he was going to enjoy this school visit.

The laboratory visit was scheduled for one morning straight after assembly. Muldoon drove the school bus to the Steinn plant. Dickinson noticed that Miss Scullery did not have much to say to the PE teacher. Perhaps they really weren't bosom buddies after all, he conceded. The thoughts of bosoms made him turn in his seat and look over his shoulder at Miss Scullery, who was well endowed in that department. She noticed his stare and raised her eyebrows.

Dickinson shook his head and grinned apologetically. He clutched the rolled up animal rights poster he had hidden under his shirt, close to his body, and nestled down in his seat, out of her view, while he planned how he intended to demonstrate to make the most impact. It would be no good just bringing out his poster and shouting his message as soon as they went through the gate. The security men would be on to him before he could get started. There had to be somewhere where he could protest to best effect. Maybe he could climb up onto a roof and make his presence felt from there. Yes that's what he'd do. Climb up on the roof like the prisoners who took to the rooftop in that Dartmoor prison protest. This was going to be a great morning. He'd be a hero at school and in the animal rights movement.

The school bus had no problems getting into the Steinn Brothers site, even though security was more obvious than usual, with three peak-capped guards manning the barrier at the entrance, instead of the usual lone figure. The bus was expected, so they were waved through after one of the guards had glanced at the teachers and given the students a perfunctory once over.

Miss Scullery left her seat, walked to the front of the bus and gave her group a lecture on what she expected from them.

"Do follow me and keep together. There will be no wandering off on your own. This is an industrial plant and there will be areas that might be dangerous."

Dickinson stuck his hand up to ask her a question.

"Dickinson?" she snorted, not pleased at being interrupted.

"If there are things I'd rather not see, Miss, can I stand just outside?"

Miss Scullery frowned at this request. Not being one of her biology group she did not know Dickinson well. She decided the boy might be a bit squeamish and reluctantly nodded agreement.

"I will lead the party, along with our official guide. Mr Muldoon will bring up the rear to ensure none of you get lost." She checked her wristwatch. "Is that clear? Any questions?" To her relief they all seemed to understand. "Right. File off the bus and wait in the car park." She left Reynard Muldoon to get them organised while she signed in at the reception office.

Eventually a young man in a white lab coat accompanied Diana Scullery back to the waiting crowd and the visit began. Barry Dickinson made sure he was the very last person in the crocodile of students. He fell into step beside Muldoon, humming happily to himself at the prospect of causing the maximum disturbance with his one-man protest. He nudged the PE teacher as they followed the other students and winked conspiratorially at him.

Out of the corner of his mouth Muldoon whispered. "Don't start until I give you the word. We need to be over near building 37 to make the maximum impact."

Dickinson frowned. How come Muldoon was so clued up about the layout of the research plant? What was the significance of building 37? He hugged his poster to his chest and bided his time.

"Please, can you all put on one of these." The young lab assistant handed out paper hair covers. "We have to avoid all possible contamination in the building we are about to tour, as this is a sterile packing department."

Reluctantly, Dickinson donned his paper hair net. He looked around the group and was struck by their laughable appearance. "Do we all have to dress up as dinner ladies?" he asked Miss Scullery.

She glared back at him from under her own white headgear and snapped her reply. "Yes!"

Dickinson followed the group, making sure he kept well back from Miss Scullery. If she latched on to him there would be no chance of a demo. Muldoon locked the doors behind them, and they caught up with the eager biology students, who had their noses pressed against the protective glass wall, which separated them from the ampoule filling process.

"What are they doing, Miss?" One eager student asked.

The white-coated guide answered the question. "These machines are filling ampoules which are used for medical injections. We pack biological products here for the overseas market."

Dickinson watched the machines automatically fill and seal the glass ampoules at a phenomenal speed. They worked tirelessly like robots, with only one operative keeping an eye on the whole process. It was impossible to tell if that person was a he or a she, under all that protective clothing. The operator walked up and down the row of machines, checking the levels of product and the supply of empty ampoules.

The biology group crowded around Miss Scullery and asked innumerable questions. Grudgingly, Dickinson had to admit she knew her stuff. She seemed to know the majority of the answers with little input from the official guide.

"Now we are going over to the cloning laboratory." The guide explained. There was a hum of interest from the biology students. Scullery glanced over at Muldoon and nodded almost imperceptibly. Only Dickinson noticed the unspoken exchange. That was only because he was bored with the ampoule filling department and was gazing around for something else to occupy his mind. I wonder what that was about? He thought.

"Steinn Brothers is one of a few firms in this country, licensed to experiment in cloning techniques." Miss Scullery told her flock. Then she smiled at the group guide and gestured with her hand, inviting him to explain in more detail.

"Quite so. We are licensed by the Department of Health to clone certain body organs to test new treatments on."

"Don't you use experimental animals?" Dickinson asked, disappointment and disbelief showing in his voice.

"We have to use laboratory animals for some tests. The government has made it a legal requirement." Knowing the delicacy of the subject and being all too aware of how often the plant was besieged by protestors, he continued. "Of course we use animals especially bred for the purpose and they are never allowed to suffer."

Barry Dickinson had just opened his mouth to argue, when Muldoon kicked the lad's shin and put his finger to his lips demanding silence. Good thinking, Dickinson acknowledged. Surprise was their best ally. No good giving his presence away at this point in the game.

"We clone specific organs, such as human cornea or mucous membranes, and use the tissue samples we produce, to check for the toxicity of our new products. We can only keep the tissue samples for a specified time, and we can only use them for an authorised purpose. Then they must be destroyed according to government guidelines."

"What about growing a human foetus? I know they have cloned a sheep, but would you be able to clone a whole human being, one day?" One of the biology students asked the inevitable question.

Dickinson rolled his eyes up to the roof and shook his head sadly.

"He's seen too much science fiction. What an anorak!" He whispered to himself.

"The short answer is yes. The technology already exists to clone a sheep, as you said. That same technology could produce a human clone. But the government will not allow scientists to play God; and quite rightly so."

The answer stunned Dickinson. He had assumed the boy who asked the question was an idiot.

Miss Scullery had a quiet word with their guide then spoke aloud to the group. "We are now going to see a cloning laboratory. It is a small unit so we will go inside in groups of four. Follow us across the yard and don't dawdle or wander off."

Dickinson shot an enquiring glance at Muldoon, who nodded to confirm that they were to follow the group.

As they crossed the yard, Rey Muldoon dug his fellow conspirator in the ribs and pointed to a large, flat roofed building to their right. Dickinson looked over at the box shaped structure and noticed the number 37 painted on the only door visible on that side of the building. That was it! That was where his PE teacher has suggested he made his protest for the maximum impact! He looked at the building for some way of climbing up onto the roof and was rewarded by the sight of a narrow metal fire escape, at the side of it.

"Now?" He fingered his poster and whispered in Muldoon's ear.

"Better wait until the last group has gone into the cloning lab." Muldoon mouthed. "I'll tell you when."

The students aligned themselves into groups of four and stood alongside the cloning laboratory wall, awaiting their turn. Dickinson made sure he was the very last in the line, a task made easy by the enthusiasm of his fellow students. Slowly each group of four entered the building and shuffled along the row of technicians working on the cloning line. The guide explained what was taking place and answered all their questions at length, even allowing each student to view a section of newly cloned tissue under a microscope.

Dickinson grew restless waiting for his chance to make a dash for building 37. Muldoon shook his head, silently counselling patience.

At last there was only the final group left to follow their fellows into the cloning lab. Dickinson felt a tug on his arm as the boy in front of him vanished through the doorway.

"Now!" Muldoon spat the order.

Dickinson ran across the empty yard and clattered up the iron steps to the roof of building 37. His quick steps rattled across the metal roofing of the building alerting the staff inside. He pulled out his animal rights poster and unrolled it. Waving the paper at arms' length he shouted his protests across the empty yard. It was not empty for long.

139

"Come down off there before you fall." Smiffy, the under zoo keeper, was the first on the scene. He had been having a cup of tea inside building 37, and was closest to the door.

Armstrong stormed out of the doorway just behind him.

"Come down, lad, before you get hurt."

The keepers were soon joined by a gaggle of white-coated workers and the security guards. Finally, Dr Steinn, the head of the research department, stormed out of the building and waved his arms furiously at the schoolboy.

While all this was going on, Muldoon took advantage of the diversion. He sprinted across the yard and slipped unnoticed into building 37's open doorway. Five minutes was all the time Dickinson managed to sustain his protest. He made the most of his chance but a young security guard, encouraged by Dr Steinn, ran across the rooftop and rugby tackled the protestor.

Dr Steinn breathed a sigh of relief once the incident was under control, but his suspicions were aroused the moment he noticed the door to building 37 was swinging open. He shouted for back up from the security guards and rushed into the building. It was all over in seconds. Reynard Muldoon was caught as he tried to search the building.

"Well? What were you doing inside building 37? This area has top security and contains some very sensitive research projects. What do you think you are doing in here?"

Muldoon spread his hands and smiled disarmingly. "I'm a teacher. I was supposed to be in charge of the students. When I saw that idiot on the roof I felt responsible. I ran in here because I thought there would be a way onto the roof from inside the building."

Dr Steinn frowned and pursed his lips. He couldn't argue with the logic of the man's explanation and it seemed innocent enough on the surface. He looked the intruder over, searching for signs of a camera, but he could see nothing suspicious.

"Shall I search him, sir?" A security man stepped forward enthusiastically.

Steinn hesitated. Maybe he was getting paranoid after the report and photograph of the Eagle-dog in the national newspaper. He considered his options, but finally he said quietly. "No, there's no need for that. This teacher is hardly one of our rivals trying to steal research secrets, is he?"

Muldoon smiled with relief and tightened his grip on the tiny spy camera and the other sample he held hidden in his left fist. He put his hand into his trouser pocket on the pretext of searching for a handkerchief and hid the camera away. Mopping his brow with the hanky, he walked away from the laboratory staff and went out into the yard.

Dickinson stood in the yard surrounded by security guards, like an escaped prisoner recaptured.

"You stupid boy!" Muldoon rounded on the lad. "You could have fallen off that roof top. As it is, the school will probably never be invited again to visit this plant. I'll sort out your punishment back at school." Watched closely by Dr Steinn and his staff, he made a show of turning the boy around and frog marching him to the car park and the empty bus.

Dickinson was confused. Muldoon had encouraged him to carry out the protest but now he was acting as if he was angry about the demonstration. Back in the bus and alone with the PE teacher, he asked. "You did suggest I demonstrated on the roof of that building, didn't you sir?"

Muldoon tapped his finger on his lips to silence the boy. "I think you must have misunderstood me, Dickinson. Anyway, no harm done. Let's forget about it, shall we?"

The boy was now completely confused. He thought back to what had been said in the yard and knew he had not misunderstood his teacher, at all. He was about to protest again when he saw Miss Scullery and the others returning to the bus. He sat down and pretended to be asleep. The least said the better, he decided. There was no trusting teachers. They were a funny lot!

Reynard Muldoon and Diana Scullery returned earlier than planned from their visit to the Steinn Brothers' plant, thanks to Dickinson's escapade. They returned the students safely to the school dining hall to wait for the first dinner session, then locked themselves in the biology prep room to discuss the events of that morning.

"Did you manage to see all you wanted?" Muldoon asked between bites of his packed lunch.

"No, but I suppose I saw all they'd let me. They seem a very secretive lot over there."

"I suppose you can't really blame them with people like young Dickinson around. Anyway since when have these criminals made the job of the bureau any easier?"

"I missed Dickinson's little escapade. Did it work out for you?"

"I managed to get into building 37 but I wasn't there long before Steinn turned up and caught me." Muldoon shrugged his shoulders and pulled a face to show his disappointment. "There was certainly some strange equipment in there. There was a container from the Boston Cryogenic Company and laid out beside it was what looked like a body bag."

"Cryogenic equipment? There's nothing illegal in that but it's not what I'd expect to find in a cloning lab." Scullery looked surprised.

"I thought that too. But as you say, it's not illegal and it's not what we are looking for. I just had time to take a few photographs of the layout and I picked up one small sample."

Scullery raised her eyebrows at this news. From the lining of his pocket, Muldoon fished a small dark coloured feather.

"Ah!" Diana grabbed the feather and put it under a microscope. "Definitely a bird of prey and a big one at that. It's probably from the neck area. DNA would confirm the species, but it's not worth sending it in to HQ for analysis. They will take months and then only confirm what we know already. It's a pretty safe bet it's an eagle feather from the Gryphon they have created. It looks as if the hybrid has been or is still in, that actual building." She moved aside to let Muldoon peer down the microscope at his find. "What do you think, agent Muldoon?"

"Oh! I agree with you, of course. You're the biology expert, Dr Scullery. I'm just the muscle in this operation."

Scullery frowned and looked at him under her knitted brow. "You and I have worked together before, Rey. I know you are not just the muscle." She sat on a stool and started to eat one of her sandwiches.

"We've got to get into area 37 unseen; preferably at night when the plant is closed. I know they will have tight security but it shouldn't be beyond me. Anyway I will get this film developed and see if it shows anything I may have missed." Rey polished an apple on his trousers and bit deeply into it.

"There's always Tony Tompkins' Uncle Albert of course. He owns the woods that grow alongside the barbed wire fence of the plant. I am moving in with Tony in a day or two. I will work on him then." Scullery told her partner.

"Watch out for that twit, Tompkins. He'll get you into bed, given half a chance." Rey told her.

"So what? Do you think I can't handle him?"

"No! I meant be careful you don't kill the little runt!"

Agent Scullery grinned broadly at her colleague's joke.

Chapter Eighteen

The morning after the excitement of Dickinson's demonstration at the Runford plant, Smiffy did not arrive at work on time. Head keeper Armstrong was incensed. It meant he had to do all the work himself, including cleaning out the Eagle-dog, which he found frightening.

"Smiffy's swinging the lead again. I'll get the office to ring his sister and chase him up." He grumbled to himself as he brewed his first cup of tea of the day and ogled the topless model in his newspaper. "He was fine yesterday. I bet there's nothing up with him. I'll sort him out, see if I don't!" He snatched the receiver off his desk telephone and reported the absence to the secretary in reception. The head keeper's mouth fell open when she explained the situation to him.

"Oh! Nobody told me Smiffy had permission to come in late. How am I supposed to run this department if people don't tell me what's going on." Armstrong's voice sank to a pleading whine.

The secretary was brisk. "I can't help you there. All I know is, Dr Steinn told me to ask Mr Smith to come into work this evening, to help him with some special job."

Armstrong let the receiver drop onto the base and sat down heavily on his chair; his mouth set in a glum line, his brow furrowed with worry. So that's how it was. Smiffy was the boss's favourite, after that episode with the Eagle-dog's injection. Without thinking, Armstrong voiced his fears aloud.

"Next thing he'll be getting promotion and he'll take my job over!"

Hearing his own voice ringing out in the empty building he clamped his hand to his mouth and swore under his breath.

Smiffy arrived at work just as Armstrong was sweeping up and getting ready to go home. "Alright for some." Armstrong grumbled as he pushed his arms into his overcoat sleeves. "Fine bloody time to start work!"

"Aye and I'll be working all night, if I know Dr Steinn." Smiffy shook his head, resigned to a busy late shift.

Armstrong cheered up visibly at the thought of Smiffy working through to the small hours of the morning. The head keeper was still grinning as he left for home. Certainly Smiffy was right be concerned about working with Steinn. There would be no tea breaks every half hour, with the doctor in charge. Armstrong almost pitied his underling, but then, remembering his fears for his own job, he muttered under his breath. "Serves you damn well right, Smiffy!

You're a little creep, sucking up to the boss like you did."

With all the day staff gone and only the security staff on duty, Dr Steinn joined Smiffy in building 37.

"Tonight we have a very important task." He told Smiffy as he locked and bolted the outside doors. "Follow me into the sluice room we have to gown up for this operation." Steinn tapped the security code into the internal door and led the way.

Smiffy was dumbstruck. He knew there were other rooms next to the sterile laboratories but they were out of bounds to him. He had never been allowed anywhere near them before.

Twenty minutes later the two men emerged, clad from head to foot in green sterile outfits. Smiffy peered from under a green hair net at Dr Steinn, who was dressed in gown, mask, hat, rubber gloves and green wellingtons, looking like a surgeon about to perform an operation.

"I'll need your help getting the body out." Steinn grunted through his mask.

Body! Smiffy panicked. Was the Eagle-dog dead? Had he killed it with that injection? Armstrong hadn't mentioned any problems. He hardly had time to consider the implications before Dr Steinn led him over to the huge stainless steel cryogenics container.

"Body!" Smiffy exclaimed aloud.

Steinn glanced at his helper and frowned. "It's only a dead body. 'It's just a frozen stiff,' as my Italian Uncle would have put it." He laughed aloud at his tasteless joke. "It can't hurt you. Here, grab hold of this chain and pull it down when I give the word."

Smiffy took hold of the chain like a man in a dream. He could see the steel links were threaded over a pulley, which was suspended on a beam, over the top of the stainless steel cryogenic tank. He watched apprehensively as Dr Steinn climbed the high steps into the roof of the building and unscrewed the top of the container. He blinked and shook his head several times, hoping he would wake up from the nightmare and find he was back in his own bed at home, and only dreaming.

"Right. Pull down gently on the chain." The doctor called from above.

Smiffy pulled very steadily, like a bell ringer on a go slow, and watched with growing horror as clouds of white vapour poured over the sides of the container and spilled onto the concrete floor, swirling around his green wellingtons. Through the mist of frozen vapour he saw a long plastic bag emerge from the depths; a plastic bag exactly the right size to hold a human body. From the shape of the bundle and from the little he could see through the bag, he was certain it was a human body!

"Is that...is that...a stiff...I mean, a body in that bag?" Smiffy stuttered.

Dr Steinn ignored his question and concentrated on guiding the steaming bag out of the cryogenic container and over a stainless steel trolley positioned below.

Smiffy gulped and closed his eyes. In the dark, in the near silence, he could hear his heart thumping and the blood rushing through his head. When he dared to raise his eyelids and look again, the plastic bag was lying on the trolley. White frost was already forming all over it.

"Come on, no dawdling. We need to move Professor Steinn to the sterile operating laboratory toute suite." Dr Steinn closed the lid on the steel container and pushed the trolley towards the sluice room. Smiffy did as he was told, moving automatically, like a man trapped in a horrible dream.

In the sterile laboratory, Dr Steinn pushed the trolley under a plastic tent and switched on a fan heater that inflated the cover with warm air.

"Now we have a lengthy wait, Smith. Maybe it would be a good time for you to make a coffee and have a biscuit."

Smiffy was out of the operating lab in the twinkling of an eye. He didn't wait for the doctor to change his mind. He made the coffee and filched two of Armstrong's ginger biscuits before shouting to the doctor. The main building had gone very chilly with the onset of evening and the liquid nitrogen that had escaped from the cryogenic container. Smiffy stirred his drink with the biscuit and watched the steam rise from his mug, but there was little comfort for him there. The steam only reminded him of the vapour rising from the body on the trolley. He went over to the thermostat that controlled the night temperature for the animals' welfare and clicked it up a notch.

Much later that night, Smiffy watched as Dr Steinn checked the temperature of the body contained within the bag. He could hear his boss talking to himself as he worked.

"Come on Uncle Enrico. Let's get you warmed up to room temperature, then I can remove your brain."

Smiffy felt sick inside, but Doctor Steinn was obviously enjoying himself. He kept his helper informed with a running commentary of all the gory details as he worked.

"I'm connecting the carotid artery and the jugular vein in the neck, to a pump circulating oxygenated Ringer's solution, warmed to human blood heat. That will flush out and replace the preserving solution they used to prevent damage to the cells at sub zero temperatures. "

Smiffy understood very little of what was said but he watched in morbid fascination as the doctor worked on his Uncle's body. It felt exactly as if he was viewing a horror movie through his fingers; he felt he daren't watch, but he just had to. The surgical procedures seemed to take forever, but finally with the cannulae firmly in place, Dr Steinn stepped back and switched on the artificial circulation pump. This time the doctor addressed his remarks to the dead body. "There you are, professor, that should soon warm up the cockles of your brain cells. If the Italian freezing boys did their job properly your old grey matter will soon be functioning properly again."

Frank Steinn left the brain to warm up to working temperature while Smiffy made them both another mug of steaming black coffee. Working so late was proving very tiring for the doctor. It had been a particularly harrowing day for him. He had conducted several disciplinary interviews with the security people about that schoolboy who had breached their systems and managed to mount his protest on the roof of building 37. Dr Steinn could have done with a good night's sleep but he daren't leave this delicate task until the day time and the arrival of the regular staff. He'd never hear the last of it if they knew he was carving up human bodies in the building.

Eventually Frank Steinn checked the progress of the procedure to revive Professor Steinn's brain. Satisfied all was going to plan, he went to fetch the apparatus he had prepared to house it. He wheeled in a glass container, which looked to Smiffy like a large round fish tank.

"It's full of the Ringers solution and has a thermostatically controlled heating coil to keep the environment at precisely the temperature of human blood. There's also a small pump to keep the solution rich in oxygen. The professor's brain will store there happily for some days, while I work out a way to communicate with it." Dr Steinn explained the finer details to his helper, being rather proud of what he had invented. Dr Steinn did not explain to Smiffy why he felt he must work on the brain in the first place. What he left unsaid was the fact that Professor Enrico Steinn had developed a technique of fusing eggs from widely differing species and growing the resulting embryo successfully to maturity. The Gryphon had been his most successful experiment so far, but Frank knew it was only the beginning. The techniques held untold promise of a scientific breakthrough, and there was a vast amount of money to be made out of the novel technology. With the capability of making novel species at will, and with Steinn Brothers' capacity to clone them, the world would be his oyster.

"Then you had to go and die on us and take your secrets with you!" Absentmindedly, Frank addressed the body on the operating table as if the Professor could actually hear him. "Well, I won't be beaten. I put millions into your research. Just when it was about to pay off, you had to have a heart attack. You never did keep records and always kept the details to yourself. That was hardly cricket, was it, Uncle!"

Gradually, over the next few hours, the head thawed out, until Dr Steinn was able to sever it from the body and remove the brain from the skull.

Smiffy closed his eyes to shut out the vision of Dr Steinn butchering the professor's carcass. He covered his ears as the electric saw sliced through the top of the skull. He would have loved an excuse to get away from the laboratory but the doctor insisted he needed his help to pass instruments and mop up the blood.

Dr Steinn worked happily on into the night until he had the brain separated from the skull and floating in a glass dish. Painstakingly, he lowered the human brain into the new home he had prepared for it, checked that all the support systems were working correctly, then covered the glass tank with a metal cover and locked it securely. Nothing could be seen of the brain floating in its cell. All that could be heard was the faint hum of the pumps and heating elements as the system performed its vital tasks.

Smiffy felt much better once the brain was out of sight and the body was covered with a green sheet. But his relief was short lived.

"Now to deal with the rest of him." Steinn said, and smiled at his helper.

Pushing the empty head between the Professor's legs, he sealed the corpse in its plastic bag. In no time he and Smiffy wheeled the body bag back into the main animal house and positioned it under a skylight in the roof and near the pulley system. Hooking the bag firmly onto the chain, Steinn directed Smiffy to use the pulley to hoist the body bag up into the roof space, where it dangled near the skylight.

"We must dispose of Uncle Enrico's remains now. I don't want any loose ends left for people to find. His body will have to go the same way we get rid of our other biological waste." Steinn explained, with about as much emotion as a housewife telling her husband to put the empty milk bottles on the step. "I will go out onto the flat roof and open the skylight. You stay here and hoist him to the very top. Pull him up when I shout."

Smiffy didn't answer. He was dumbstruck. Wasn't it illegal to be disposing of dead bodies? Didn't they imprison body snatchers? Then on the other hand, he assured himself, the old man had died a natural death and had already been frozen, so I suppose he had already been disposed of, in a way. Smiffy didn't really know what to think, but he wasn't going to argue with the doctor.

"Alright! Pull on the chain." Dr Steinn shouted from above him. Smiffy did as he was told.

"OK, Smith. I've managed to get Uncle Enrico on the roof. Now you must come up here and help me to carry him."

Reluctantly, Smiffy climbed the iron fire escape to the roof and made his way towards Dr Steinn's torchlight. In the pale glow from the torch and by the faint light from the new moon sailing overhead, he could just make out the green robed figure of the doctor. Lying beside him was the bulky plastic bag.

"Give me a hand. We need to drag Uncle Enrico to the edge of the roof, above the caustic tank. Then we can tip him into it." Steinn pointed to their destination.

"Caustic tank?" Smiffy repeated. "Surely that's sealed with a metal lid. He'll bounce on the lid!"

"Usually it is, but I took the lid off earlier, just to

save ourselves that very problem. The sides are at least ten feet high; we'd have had a hell of a job bodily lifting Enrico over the side, from the yard."

Bodily lifting! Smiffy thought, aghast. That was exactly what they were doing; lifting a body! He was sure that disposing of bodies must be some sort of an offence. Didn't undertakers have to do a night school course or something, to make it legal?

"Are you sure we can do this, legally?" Smiffy heard his own timorous tones questioning his boss.

"What's illegal about it. He's certified dead. It's no different from burning him in a crematorium or letting him rot underground, surely?"

Smiffy just shrugged his shoulders. He had detected the aggressive note in Steinn's voice and knew it was dangerous to argue. He grabbed one end of the plastic bag. Between them they dragged it to the edge of the roof. Steinn shone his torch down into the yard. The beam reflected back from the bubbling surface of the caustic soda solution in the tank.

"Hold your end up in the air, while I cut through the bottom of the bag." Steinn slashed across the bag with a scalpel.

Smiffy felt the body and head slide out of the plastic tube and heard them splash into the tank below him. He didn't particularly want to look down but his eyes were drawn to the caustic solution, in spite of his revulsion. He saw the body sink slowly beneath the surface like a man in quicksand. With a final macabre wave of one pale hand, Professor

Steinn's corpse sank to its final resting place. The ripples on the surface of the caustic solution flattened out until the reflection of the moon rode smoothly among the bubbles of fat.

"Good, that's got rid of the evidence. It'll be completely dissolved in day or two." Dr Steinn said cheerfully. "Now we can clear up before we call it a night."

Smiffy just stood on the rooftop looking down at the caustic tank, and shook his head sadly.

"What's the problem?" Steinn asked.

"Didn't he have himself frozen because he expected to be revived at some time in the future?"

"Humph! Lot of nonsense! The personality resides in the brain. You, or I for that matter, are just the sum total of our memories. I've started to revive his brain, so what more could he want. By tomorrow he will be alive again; in a fashion." Steinn walked away across the roof of building 37 and clattered down the cast iron fire escape, leaving the brain in its survival tank in a side room off the laboratory. It was almost 4am before they could change out of their operating gowns and head for home.

It had been a tiring night for Frank Steinn, especially as he had undertaken the complicated surgical work alone, but he was pleased with the outcome so far. Now he had to find a way to tap into the activity of the revived brain and learn the professor's secrets. He rubbed his tired eyes and stared at his helper. "Enough is enough...Sufficient unto the day…" He muttered wearily. "Oh by the way! Don't mention any of this to anyone, Smith. I would be very upset indeed if it got out." Smiffy was left in no doubt he meant it. That last comment was delivered with such venom.

As dawn broke with a rosy glow over the fens and the sliver of the new moon paled into insignificance, Dr Steinn drove his Jaguar past the security guards and out of the research site. He accelerated along Beggars Bush Lane and onto the A16 heading for home.

"Tomorrow will be a busy day." he told himself. "Tomorrow I must search the Internet for papers on the use of brain electrodes. I do remember seeing the Americans have published a paper on the subject only recently."

Smiffy pedalled his bicycle, following the doctor's car along Beggars Bush Lane, before he turned towards Runford. What an awful night he had had. His mind was full of headless bodies and disembodied brains. A thin veil of morning mist filled the dykes that skirted the ploughed fields and spilled over onto the road. Smiffy pedalled as fast as he could to get away from that unwelcome reminder of his night's work. He had been sworn to secrecy and promised a huge bonus for his help, but he'd have gladly forgone any monetary reward to regain his peace of mind.

Chapter Nineteen

Albert Williams had worked hard at his studies. He hardly left the house after his return from Macclesfield, making only a few quick trips to the corner shop to stock up on essentials like food and drink. Eventually, even his thirst for learning had to pale, being housebound became too much for an outdoor loving countryman. He'd never spent so much time indoors since his school days. He found himself reading the same lines again and again and none of the information was going into his memory. He longed for the open air and the freedom of the countryside.

"All work and no play..." Albert muttered to himself, and decided there would be no harm in a short rest from his studies and a trip to his woods to blow away the cobwebs. He still harboured a strong desire to try and raise the Gryphon again. He gathered together the equipment he would need for another attempt at raising the beast, and drove to Beggars Bush wood, where he changed into his druid outfit in the privacy of his truck.

Dressed in his white towelling robe and carrying a pair of sacrificial lamb chops, he set off through the trees to his oak grove, whistling as he went, happy to be out in the fresh air again. At the oak grove, he found everything was as he had left it. The blood stained altar stone was still in place and the grass still bore traces of being flattened, where he, Tony and Diana had conducted the last ceremony. He cut up the chops with his bronze knife and set out the sacrifice in the prescribed manner. Dropping onto his knees before the altar, Pollawsdoc started his chanting. The trees seemed to whisper in the wind, exactly as they had before, but nothing else happened. Even after he had finished the ceremony, there was no sign of the Gryphon. There was not even a visit from a passing carrion crow. Albert was extremely disappointed. This time he could not use his nephew's scepticism as an excuse for failure. He knew success or failure was all down to himself. Unwilling to accept defeat, he decided to try some of his new skills. Kneeling on one knee, he closed his eyes and concentrated all his thoughts on the Gryphon, trying to reach out towards it with his mind. Surely, the lessons he had learned from the Wise One must be of some use in such a situation.

After some minutes, Albert began to feel he was not alone. He opened his eyes to check. He could see no visible change in the woods around him, yet he still felt a presence was not too far away from him. Albert redoubled his efforts, asking the beast for some sign to show it really was nearby.

For several minutes he maintained his level of concentration, but nothing happened, and he was beginning to feel mentally exhausted.

"Come on! Just one small sign. I know you're there." He muttered to himself. There was a strange answering scream in the distance; a shrill shriek like the cry of a bird of prey!

Albert jumped, and looked around him, startled by the noise, but completely thrilled. He was sure that cry had been in answer to his call. As he stood looking around the woods, the cry came again. Albert turned quickly to locate the direction of the sound and found he was looking towards the barbed wire perimeter fence of the Steinn Brothers research plant.

"So that's where you are, my beauty." He whispered the words to himself in triumph. "Maybe you're trapped or caged and can't fly over here." Steinn Brothers have no business interfering with my Gryphon, he thought angrily.

Albert walked the short distance to the perimeter fence and pressed his face close to the wire. Through the diamond mesh he had a clear view into the compound but he could see nothing but the brick walls that formed the backs of buildings. There was nowhere visible from the woods that looked to be a likely hiding place for his Gryphon. Disappointed he paced up and down that stretch of the perimeter fence trying to decide what to do next.

"I'm certain it's in there." he muttered to himself. "Maybe I should try and make mental contact again."

He stood against the wire, his head bowed, his outstretched hands clutching the fence. He lowered his chin onto his chest, closed his eyes and concentrated on contacting the beast by telepathy. The druid focused his thoughts hard, so hard he clenched his fingers and bent the wire mesh out of shape. There was a harsh birdlike cry from somewhere in the compound.

"That settles it!" Albert stamped his foot in frustration. "I'll have to get in there to find it."

Inside the chemical plant, security was on full alert. The roasting they had been given by Dr Steinn, over Dickinson's animal rights demonstration, was still fresh in their minds. They were on permanent Red Alert. One of the guards noticed the strange white figure in the towelling dressing gown as soon as it started to pace up and down beside the fence.

By the time Albert had gripped the wire and given his full attention to contacting the Gryphon, there were several pairs of curious eyes concentrating on him.

"He looks to be a harmless old man, but you never can tell with cranks like that. Keep a constant check on him and report to me if he does anything suspicious." The head of security went back to his office and his morning coffee, confident the high fence would keep out any old crank.

Albert eyed the high fence, wondering how he could scale it and get over the razor wire coiled on the top. There was no chance he could just climb over, even less chance he could jump that high. It was all of fifteen feet high and had no weak points. The compound seemed deserted. He stepped back into the shadow of the woods and gave the problem some thought.

"No use presenting myself at the front gate. They have more security there than Fort Knox!" He drummed his fingers against his thigh while he considered the problem. A sudden thought struck him and he smiled. "If I was younger I could try pole vaulting it, I suppose." He shrugged his shoulders. "But I'm not...There has to be a way over. What would the Wise One do in these circumstances?" Suddenly the thought of Enoesiw gave him an idea. "Levitation! I could try levitation!"

Albert had only just started studying the art of levitation in his druid lessons. He had half-heartedly practised some of the preliminary exercises in reducing his weight but had never achieved complete weightlessness or managed to leave the ground. When he had first read the exercises he had been only mildly curious about defying gravity. At first, the idea had frightened him a little. Now he had a good reason to learn the secret of levitation. Even though he knew it was stupid for someone so inexperienced to try flying unaided, his mind wouldn't let go of the idea.

"I'll go home and concentrate just on that one thing." The determination in his voice was almost tangible.

Back home, Albert skipped lunch and went straight up to his inner sanctum; the empty back bedroom he had designated his study. He sat cross legged on the linoleum and settled himself in the lotus position. Then he tried to make contact with the Wise One.

Eventually, by mid afternoon, he had reached his teacher's mind, even though the answers were intermittent and the contact spasmodic.

'Why do you want…learn levitation so early…your training? …dangerous…' The message was broken but understandable.

Pollawsdoc tried to explain the urgency of locating the Gryphon.

'…Gryphon…?' The reply was incoherent.

Albert made a supreme effort to empty his mind of all extraneous thoughts and tried again. This time the Wise One must have got the message for he started transmitting the visualisation exercises to achieve weightlessness. He concentrated on the instructions as he had never concentrated before. Gradually he began to feel distinctly lighter.

By teatime Albert had mastered the first stages of levitation and began to feel his buttocks lifting off the linoleum. He opened his eyes in astonishment and immediately thumped back onto the floor.

"Yes!" He punched the air with his clenched fist. "I did it!"

The Wise One, who was more or less following his students progress via the intermittent mental images, was thrilled for him.'Pollawsdoc, that was stupendous enough for one day.'

Albert was exhausted but defiant. He asked his teacher why he had to stop.

'...Mavis Harbottle...double D bra...Besides you've skipped lunch...light headed.' The warning came through soft and very unclear, but Albert got the message.

'Can we try again tomorrow?' Albert pleaded.

'... I have a hospital appointment...' The Wise One sounded extremely tired and very old.

Next day Albert practised all he had learned and was thrilled to find he had not lost the knack of making himself more or less weightless. Twice he hovered inches above the linoleum before he thumped back onto the bedroom floor again but the concentration necessary to maintain the weightless state for any length of time was still beyond his reach. He now appreciated what the Wise One had achieved and he marvelled at the man's tenacity to rise over thirty feet into the air. By mid day he had given himself a splitting headache by trying too hard. He had to stop for a rest and egg and chips.

Chapter Twenty

Dr Steinn was full of enthusiasm when he returned to the Beggars Bush plant. He had spent a whole day surfing the internet to find the information he wanted. It would only be a matter of hours before he inserted electrodes into the brain of Professor Enrico Steinn and got it to reveal the secrets of creating creatures like the Gryphon. Having warned his secretary he was not to be disturbed on any account, he made his way to building 37.

"Eh up! Here comes Steinn." Armstrong sounded the warning, pushed his newspaper into a drawer, slid his coffee mug under his desk and picked up a broom.

Smiffy looked petrified. He hadn't slept properly since he'd worked right through the night with the doctor.

"If he asks for me, I'm not here." He raced to the far end of the building and shut himself in one of the empty animal cages.

"Morning, Armstrong." Dr Steinn sounded full of the joys. "I'm working in the sterile laboratory and I'm not to be disturbed. Not for anything." He opened the security door with the secret code and vanished from sight, slamming the door shut behind him.

"You can come out now, Smiffy. He's gone."

Smiffy left his hiding place and sauntered back to his boss, whistling nonchalantly.

"He's got you worried, hasn't he. What's been going on? You've not been the same man since you worked overnight."

Smiffy shrugged his shoulders. Dr Steinn's warning about keeping quiet was uppermost in his mind. "Nothing, honestly. I just ain't sleeping well. That's all"

Armstrong was surprisingly sympathetic. "I've heard night work can upset your biological clock." He said knowledgeably, then he added with a touch of his usual sarcasm. "Mind you, it don't usually happen after just one late night."

Smiffy shrugged his shoulders again, but said nothing.

Dr Steinn unlocked the cover he had placed around the glass tank containing the thawed out brain and checked the circulation of the Ringers solution. Everything seemed to be going to plan. He prepared several platinum probes and studied the brain surface under a low magnification microscope to ascertain were they were to be inserted.

By mid morning Dr Steinn had attached all the wires to the brain and plugged them into his laptop computer. Now he was ready to make contact with his dead uncle.

He switched on the laptop and typed in a request.

'Is anybody there? Are you receiving me, Uncle Enrico?' He sat back and waited for a reply. Fifteen painfully slow minutes ticked by, but nothing showed up on the computer screen to encourage the doctor.

'Come on Professor. I know you can hear me. I want to talk to you about the Gryphon project.' Steinn typed again and waited, but still nothing happened to show he was making contact. He paced the floor impatiently. This was going to be harder than he had anticipated.

By early afternoon Dr Steinn was in a rage, but he gritted his teeth and carried on trying to contact the Professor.

'Are you there, professor?' He typed in for the hundredth time. 'Is any body there?' He tried in frustration. There was a faint blip then a message came on the screen!

'No! No body is here. Get lost, nephew!'

Steinn was elated at this success. He jumped up from his chair and accidentally dropped the laptop computer. It crashed onto the floor and the screen went blank.

"God! Why me? I think that stupid brain did it on purpose!" He grabbed the computer and banged it hard on the desktop then he turned to the brain, seething with temper.

"Don't just float there doing nothing, help me!" But the professor's brain remained motionless in the Ringers solution, like a dead jellyfish in an aquarium.

"Smith!" Steinn shouted for the zoo keeper, as he was the only person he dared trust. If he had stopped to think, he was fully aware that no one could hear him shouting through the security door, but he was beyond reason. He stamped to the security door, threw it open and bellowed again at the top of his voice. "Smith, don't ignore me, man! Come here and help."

Smiffy had just picked up a full mug of coffee and dipped a ginger biscuit in it. He dropped both in fright, spilling the steaming drink all over Armstrong's desk. "Oh my God! He wants me again! Don't let him get me."

"You shouldn't be so bloody popular." Armstrong said sarcastically, and pushed him towards the open doorway.

Smiffy shuffled towards the doctor, like a man going to his own funeral.

"Ah Smith! You remember what we were doing together the other night."

Smiffy nodded vigorously. How could he ever forget.

"I need your help again." Steinn led his unwilling assistant to the glass tank containing the brain. "I have to fetch another laptop computer from my office. I haven't time to cover this over again. You must stand guard over the professor here, and make sure no one enters this room. Is that clear?"

Smiffy nodded dumbly.

"I will not be long." Steinn walked briskly out of the laboratory. The animal keeper heard the connecting door close with a bang.

Smiffy stood near the door, as far away from the floating brain as he could get, and whistled tunelessly to himself. The room seemed over warm and humid, with only the mechanical hum of the pumps and the clicking of the heating elements, breaking the silence. His imagination worked overtime. He imagined all kinds of things were happening. Out of the corner of his eye he was sure he saw the brain move in its watery environment. He turned sharply to focus on it, but he could detect no further movement.

"Is...are you... there, professor?" Smiffy asked the question hesitantly, more to assure himself that no one was there, than to actually elicit an answer.

The lap top hummed into life and bleeped as a message appeared across the screen, typed by an unseen hand.

'Yes, I'm here. Who is that?'

Smiffy's eyes nearly popped out of his head. His mouth went dry and his legs turned limp. He flopped into the chair beside the computer and buried his head in his hands.

Bleep! The sound of the laptop working again, roused him from his trance.

'Who is that? Not my awful nephew I hope.'

"No sir…Its Smith…the under zoo keeper." Smiffy laboriously typed his answer then turned and smiled at the brain. Immediately he wiped the smile from his face, feeling very stupid as he realised the thing probably couldn't see him anyway.

'Tell Dr Steinn I will not co-operate with him while I'm stuck in this tank like a jelly in limbo! Put me back into my body and I might just think about it.'

Smiffy was about to tell the professor that his body was in the caustic tank and probably all dissolved, when Dr Steinn returned.

"Everything OK, Smith? Are you feeling alright?" The doctor had noticed his helper was sitting down and looking very pale.

Smiffy couldn't speak, but he pointed dumbly at the messages on the laptop.

"Ah! Success." Steinn was elated at this sign of further contact, until he read the actual words. "Oh my God! Now what can I do?"

The laptop bleeped again. 'Welcome back nephew. I'll tell you what you can do. You can put my brain back into my body before we go any further. That's all I have to say to you.' Then the screen went blank.

Chapter Twenty One

Tony Tompkins was beside himself with delight. Diana Scullery had arranged to move in with him, that afternoon after school. He rushed home and checked the state of the spare bedroom. It had been newly papered and furnished tastefully from the second hand furniture dealers. All was tidy and welcoming, but just to make sure, he bought a bunch of flowers and put them in a milk bottle on the dressing table. Once he was convinced the room was looking good he retired to the wardrobe in his own room and checked the view through the spy hole he had installed.

Just as he was polishing the lens on his side of the partition wall he heard the sound of a key turning in the front door. Footsteps came up the stairs. She'd arrived! He dashed out of the wardrobe, entangling his arms in the clothes and knocking down the metal hangers in a heap, in his haste.

Tony threw the clothes onto the wardrobe floor and rushed to his bedroom door. He hesitated for a second to check his appearance in his dressing table mirror. Flattening his hair with his hand and switching on his best smile, he opened the door and stepped onto the landing.

"Hello Di…!" The words died in his throat as he came face to chest with Muldoon, standing so close on the narrow landing he towered over Tony.

"Oh! Hello Tompkins. I'm just helping Miss Scullery up stairs with her suitcases. God knows what she's put in them! They are heavy." Reynard Muldoon vanished into the next bedroom bearing a large suitcase in each hand.

Tony frowned. What was that gorilla of a PE teacher doing sniffing around his lodger?

"Hello Tony. Sorry if I disturbed you." Diana followed Rey up the stairs, her arms full of carrier bags and dresses on hangers.

"No. No trouble…I was just going down to make a cup of tea. Do you need a hand?"

Muldoon came out of the bedroom door as Tony offered his help. "You're a bit too late, Tompkins. It's all been carried up stairs now. And yes, I would love a cup of tea."

Tony went down to the kitchen and boiled the kettle. He had made the tea and opened a packet of biscuits long before Diana and Rey came down the stairs, whispering together. Tony was rather put out by Muldoon's arrival and this further evidence of their friendly manner towards each other. He was inclined to regard Muldoon as a rival for Diana's affection.

"All sorted out, then?" Tony asked with false bonhomie.

"Yes, thanks to Mr Muldoon here."

Tony felt a pang of jealousy at these words of thanks, but noticing the formal use of the PE teacher's name, he relaxed. He needn't worry, she wasn't even on first name terms with him yet. Probably there was no reason to get worried about him. Maybe Muldoon had heard in the staff room that Diana was moving and had just acted the gentleman.   He certainly saved me the bother of carting that heavy stuff up those steep stairs, Tony thought, smugly.

They drank their tea and Muldoon left, leaving Tony with the delectable Miss Scullery.

"Well I'll sort out my cases then I could do with a bath. If that's OK?" Diana rinsed the teacups under the hot tap and put them on the draining board to dry.

"Of course. Please yourself. I had a shower when I got in and there's plenty of hot water. I'll be in my room if you want me. I have some work to mark."

Tony was delighted with her suggestion. He couldn't have planned it better himself for it meant he could try out his surveillance equipment for real. He waited until she had gone up to her room then went into his own and bolted the door. Hastily hanging the clothes back onto their hangers to clear a space, he climbed into the wardrobe.

Inside the confined space, he pulled the door shut behind him to cut out any stray light and ensure he could get a better view through the spy hole. He positioned himself with his right eye against the lens and peered into Diana's bedroom. She was busy

174

unpacking clothes and books, putting them away in the cupboard and the chest of drawers. He could see her full length when she was working on the far side of the room and her blonde head in much greater detail when she approached her wardrobe on the partition wall between the two bedrooms.

"Come on girl, come on! Get your things unpacked then unpack yourself!" Tony whispered to himself, urging her to start stripping off for her bath. Finally she pushed a bundle under the mattress and straightened the bed again. Tony thought nothing of this as he had frequently hidden his girlie magazines under his own mattress when his mother was due to clean his room. At last she stood by the chair near the bed head and started to peel off her clothes.

Tony pushed his right eye hard against the lens, not wishing to miss one second of the strip show.

Diana took her time undressing, raising his blood pressure even more. She rolled down her tights and undid her bra, to reveal a firm pair of ample breasts.

"God I'd lose my concentration and stop levitating for the sight of those boobs!" Tony whispered.

Diana pulled down her silk knickers with her back towards him, revealing a beautifully rounded pair of firm buttocks. Finally, having tantalised him with glimpses of her naked back she turned to give him a brief full frontal pose as she donned her dressing gown.

"Well she's certainly a natural blonde!" he chuckled. The strip show ended abruptly as she put on a dressing gown and searched in her suitcase for a bath towel.

"Damn!" He was disappointed that she had been so quick. But then, he consoled himself, with any luck that spectacle will be showing nightly at a wardrobe near me!

As Diana pulled a large bath towel out of her suitcase, something small and black fell onto the floor with a loud thud. He saw her mouth an oath to herself and bend down to retrieve the fallen object, her curvaceous backside clad in towelling, angled towards him.

"Why didn't you bend down like that before you put that bloody dressing gown on?" It was a rhetorical question, muttered to himself to release his frustration.

"Good God!" Tony nearly spoke out loud, when he realised what she had dropped. He saw she had picked up a pistol and was pointing the barrel in his direction as she checked for damage. He turned away from his viewer, not sure what to think. What would a law abiding biology teacher want with an automatic pistol? It looked just like the model James Bond used on screen. He looked again trying to convince himself it was a plastic replica, but there was something about the professional way she handled it, and the obvious weight in her hand that convinced him it was the real thing. Suddenly all thoughts of cheap thrills were gone. Diana Scullery was obviously not a woman to mess with. He would have to mind his step.

Diana secreted the gun under the mattress, pushing it into the leather holster she had in the other package, then she moved out of his sight towards the bedroom door.

Tony heard the door open and close. Her footsteps could be heard going along the landing and into the bathroom. Within minutes he could hear the bath water running and Diana singing. Now was the time to make himself scarce.

Turning slowly so as not to disturb the coat hangers again, Tony pushed on the wardrobe door. Nothing happened! There was complete resistance to his urgent pushing. The door had locked behind him when he had pulled it shut. There was no catch inside the door. He was trapped!

At first Tony panicked. Locked inside the dark cupboard with hardly enough room to turn around. He felt it was airless, a feeling not helped by the musty smell rising from a pile of his dirty underwear, sweaty socks and sports shoes, tangled around his feet. Finally, all hot and bothered, he stopped struggling and tried to work out the best way to escape.

Tony knew he couldn't ask Diana for help. That would have begged the question of what he was doing in the wardrobe in the first place and probably aroused her suspicions. An irate female with a gun was the last thing he wanted to confront. He tried applying all his weight on the wardrobe door and bracing his back against the wall. He could just make out a chink of light around the top edge of the door as it took the strain.

"Damn these old wardrobes! They built them like brick shit houses! They made them too well." His mother had bought that particular piece of furniture at the local saleroom. It was made of solid oak. He pushed harder but nothing gave way.

"Oh to Hell with it!" Tony lost his temper and flung all his weight against the door. There was a loud crash as the wardrobe toppled over and fell across the end of his bed!

Tony held his breath and listened, praying that his new lodger had not heard the commotion. He was certain the noise would have alerted a deaf man, but as she was locked in the bathroom and singing to herself, he hoped he'd been lucky and escaped detection. Lying prone and at an angle, covered in loose clothes and metal coat hangers, with his arms pinned at his sides and his body trapped against the door, he could hardly move. He pressed his ear against the crack of light and listened intently. From far off he could hear Diana's sweet voice singing a selection from the Sound of Music.

"Not the singing nuns!" He growled. "They get everywhere!" In his predicament he would have grumbled at any melody.

Lying helpless at an acute incline, Tony had time to stop to think and take stock of his situation. He realised the back of the wardrobe, which now faced up to the bedroom ceiling, was made of thinner panels of wood and was probably his best means of escape. He felt among the jumble of coats and shirts that lay around him, searching for anything he could use as a tool to prise his prison open.

"Eureka!" He found a small knife in a jacket pocket. He opened the narrow blade and inserted it between the plywood backing and the oak side of the wardrobe. It was hard work and the air in the cupboard was getting even staler, but he persevered and managed to prise the backing slightly open so that he could see his bedroom wall through the narrow gap. Bracing his back against the door he bent his knees up to his chest and wedged his shoe heels against the plywood. He pushed upwards with all his strength. There was aloud crack as the bulging back started to part from the oak side and the screws sprung out.

"Tony, are you alright in there?" Diana tapped lightly on his bedroom door as she made her way back to her room. "I heard a loud bang, as if something fell over. Are you OK?"

"Damn!" He muttered under his breath. "She did hear me fall." Pushing his face close to the gap in the cupboard, he shouted back to her. "I'm fine. Just moving the furniture to make more room."

"Oh, alright. When I get changed I'm going to make myself a meal. Anything I can tempt you with? Do you fancy anything while I'm at it?"

You certainly do tempt me and I did fancy a lot of things until I got stuck in here, he thought glumly, then he had a sobering thought as he remembered the gun. He answered quickly.

"No thanks, Diana. I'll sort myself out later." He heard her footsteps pad along the landing and the door to her bedroom open and close. She would soon be taking off her dressing gown and getting dressed again. He had a sudden vision of her, all pink and powdered, but somehow he couldn't raise any enthusiasm. With the discovery of her gun, he'd temporarily lost all interest in being a Peeping Tom.

Once he had heard the girl go down stairs and he hoped she was busy in the kitchen, he kicked hard at the wood backing to his prison. The panel of oak flew off the wardrobe, letting in a breath of much needed fresh air. Tony climbed out of his coffin, and blinked in the daylight, feeling like a vampire, who had got up too early. He pushed the wardrobe upright and hammered the back on loosely with his shoe heel. He pushed the wardrobe upright against the wall, realigning the back with his spy hole. He didn't bother to open the mirrored door and attempt to tidy up the mess he knew was waiting inside. He had had enough of wardrobes. Grabbing his jacket he hurried down the stairs.

"You OK, Tony? You sound out of breath. Sure you don't fancy something?" Diana called from the kitchen.

"I'm fine. Just going to see my Uncle Albert." He left the house and made for the pub to drown his sorrows.

The Duck and Dumpling was empty of customers as it was only early evening. Tony had hoped Albert would be there but he was disappointed. He ordered a pint and checked with the barman.

"No. Not seen Albert for days. He must be damn busy to keep missing his regular morning drink. What's he up to these days?" Paddy carried on polishing the beer glasses as he spoke.

Tony ignored the question and picked up the newspaper, which he carried with his pint to a corner table. There he immersed himself in the football pages and tried to forget his recent unfortunate experience. By the time he had downed his second pint, he felt more positive, in spite of the teething problems. The locked wardrobe door and even the sight of that gun no longer bothered him. He felt he should be pleased with the success of his plan. Just a few wrinkles to iron out and he would enjoy the view of the spare bedroom. Tony mellowed as more beer went down. He was about to go home when Albert turned up.

"Tony, boy! Glad to see you. What are you having?" Albert was pleased to see his nephew.

"Well, I was just going. Maybe if you twist my arm I'll have another half." Tony sat back in his chair and waited for his uncle to join him.

When they were both seated Tony asked. "How are the druid lessons going? Having any success?"

Albert wiped the froth from his top lip and smiled broadly. "Yes. I am doing fine. I've made contact with the Wise One by telepathy and it's going well."

Tony tried to look happy for the old man, without smiling too much and giving his real feelings away. Who was Albert kidding? Himself most probably!

"Anyway I want to talk about something else."

Tony nodded, encouraging Albert to go on.

"I tried to raise that Gryphon again, but it wasn't having any."

Again Tony nodded. He said nothing but he thought a lot. With hindsight he doubted if the mythical beast had been anything but a figment of his Uncle's overactive imagination.

`"I'm sure it's trapped in the Steinn factory somewhere."

Tony sat up and took notice. "Why do you think that? Have you seen it through the wire?"

"Well, not exactly. I tried to communicate with it by telepathy and it answered from over the fence."

"You say it answered you? You mean it can talk?" Tony eyebrows shot up to his hairline.

"Don't be daft, boy! It screeched just like an eagle. I would have climbed the fence and looked for it but it's too high and too dangerous with that razor wire coiled along the top."

Tony kept his own counsel and sipped his half in silence. First that goon Muldoon had turned up with Diana. Then she had produced the gun and he had got stuck in the wardrobe. Now Albert was telling him he was making mental contact with a non-existent Gryphon, who was actually answering him back! It had been a very peculiar day.

Albert's voice broke into his nephew's thoughts. "Come round tomorrow night on your way home from school. I want to show you how I'm getting on with the levitation."

Tony nodded vaguely, drained his glass and went home.

Chapter Twenty Two

Dr Frank Steinn was having problems harnessing his Uncle's brain to his laptop computer. He could see no technical reason for this failure, but still the old man refused to communicate with him.

"I suppose it has a mind if its own!" He quipped, to relieve the tension, but in reality he was in no laughing mood.

The brain was devastated to find itself conscious but devoid of its body. When the professor had asked to be frozen on his deathbed, he had hoped to be revived and returned to good health, at some time in the future, when advances in medical science made that possible. Now all his hopes had been dashed. He could see no future for himself as a bodiless mind.

To make the situation worse, Doctor Steinn had dumped the professor's body in the vat of caustic soda he used to destroy unwanted biological waste from the research department. Although the professor was unaware of it, there was no chance of his brain being rejoined to his own body. It was fortunate for the Doctor's plans that Uncle Enrico was unaware of that fact.

Of course, Dr Steinn had no intention of informing his uncle's brain about the loss of its body. He realised he had been too hasty destroying it, but he had not reckoned on the dead professor being so belligerent. The professor was capable of ruining all his plans, even though he was only a brain in a tank of Ringers solution.

"I'll have to kid him along his body is still in the cryogenic tank." The Doctor talked to himself as he drove his Jaguar in to work. It was imperative he worked out a strategy to get the information he needed from the professor's memory.

"It's not as if he can go looking for his body." Dr Steinn chuckled at his own macabre humour and switched on the car radio.

'I ain't got nobody...' the radio crooner sang. Doctor Steinn joined in with gusto.

At the laboratory that day, the Doctor intended to prepare the brain for another question and answer session, but first he had something urgent to do.

"Armstrong! Where's that under keeper of yours. Smith, isn't it?"

Armstrong heard his name being called and automatically reached out for a broom. He always felt safer with some sort of protection when he heard Dr Steinn shout his name like that. When he realised it was Smiffy who was needed, he breathed a sigh of relief and rushed to find the under keeper.

"Smiffy, Steinn wants a word with you again."

The under keeper had hidden in the Gryphon's cage when he saw the doctor first enter the building.

"I'm busy. Won't you do?" Smiffy asked hopefully.

"No. I'm not his blue eyed boy, am I!" The head keeper couldn't resist that sarcastic comment.

Smiffy reluctantly let himself out of the Gryphon's cage and went to see what the Doctor wanted.

"Ah! Smith." Dr Steinn beamed at his helper and put his arm around the man's shoulders.

Smiffy backed away, as alarmed at this show of affection as he would have been at the embrace of a grizzly bear.

"I want to talk to you about my uncle, the professor. I need you to promise me, you will not mention what happened to the old man's body." He patted Smiffy's back like a mother burping a baby. "Not to anyone, you understand? I think we will let everyone think the body is still safe in the liquid nitrogen."

"Anyone? Who's anyone?" Smiffy was trying to visualise how he was likely to drop that fact into a casual conversation and who would be interested.

"Anyone!" The friendly tone in the Doctor's voice changed to one of menace. "Especially that brain!" He thumped Smiffy on the back, just a little too hard for comfort. Turning abruptly, he walked to the security door that led into the sterile area of the laboratory, leaving Smiffy open mouthed, in the animal house.

"By the way. I may need you to help me again, so don't go far away." That was the Doctor's parting comment as he closed the security doors.

Armstrong was hovering nearby, trying to look busy and uninterested, but dying to know exactly what was going on. "Anyone? What was he saying about anyone?"

Smiffy gulped hard. This was his first test. "Anyone? .Ah yes, anyone....He was saying ...you did your job as well as...anyone could."

Suitably flattered, Armstrong smiled and offered to make them both a mug of tea.

Inside the sterile laboratory, Doctor Steinn, renewed the connections from his portable computer to the Professor's brain. He flexed his fingers nervously like a concert pianist about to tackle an impossible Chopin concerto, and considered what message to key into his laptop. He decided to adopt a softly, softly, approach and try to charm the information out of the old man.

'Good morning, Uncle. Hope you slept well.'

The brain ignored him.

'It's your favourite nephew, Frank. You're in England now, safe with your family. Now, let's talk about the Gryphon experiment. You'll be pleased to hear it's doing fine. In fact I am reducing the dose of compound 104 and it will soon be entirely independent of any medication. You did a marvellous job there.'

'Don't expect me to clap! I'm armless!'

'Oh! Good one, Uncle Enrico! Armless, as opposed to harmless. Brilliant pun.'

'You bloody young fool! I am not in a joking mood. Either you reconnect me to my body and refreeze me, or we have nothing to discuss. I know what you're after. You want the details of the embryo joining process. Then you'll have no further use for me. Well you can want. There's nothing put down in writing about my methods. It's all stored in my memory. I don't trust you. No body, no information!'

Frank was seething but his anger was useless against the old man, and he knew it.

"Why oh why did I dump that body in the caustic?" He muttered aloud.

'Did you speak to me? What body is that?' The brain typed on the computer.

Frank was aghast, he'd forgotten the brain could hear and understand him! The Ringers solution must be transmitting the sound waves to the hearing receptors in the inner ears. He would have to keep that animal keeper well away from the laboratory in case he let slip what had happened. Things were becoming much more complicated than he had anticipated.

Chapter Twenty Three

After Albert had talked to Tony in the pub, he went home and read his druid lessons until bed time. He took a whisky night- cap, but he couldn't get any rest. His overactive mind would not let him sleep while the Gryphon was still lost.

Lying on his back, he stared at the ceiling, wondering about those answering cries he had heard from the depths of the Steinn research plant. Those calls alone convinced him the mythical animal was in the plant somewhere. The more he thought about it the more he was certain the beast was imprisoned or trapped and unable to answer his summons when he performed the sacrificial ceremony. He saw the barbed wire fence was the main obstacle to his search. Surely his new found powers could help him scale the fence and rescue the animal.

"If only I could levitate to that height, like William Arthur Cobbold did. I could rise above that fence and come down on the other side." This idea excited him so much, there was no way he could get to sleep. The more he considered it the more wide awake he became. Finally he got up, put on his towelling dressing gown and looked at his levitation exercises again.

Albert studied all night. By morning he had perfected weightlessness. Each time he sat in the lotus position and visualised himself rising into the air, he felt himself leave the floor and hover inches above the linoleum, but concentrate as hard as he could, there was no way he could make his body rise any further. It was frustrating for him, but those few inches of lift off were all he could manage. He found it very disappointing for he knew if he could levitate just fifteen feet in the air, he could have easily cleared the barbed wire fence.

At eight o'clock next morning Albert made himself a pot of strong tea and tried to contact the Wise One by ESP. He failed completely. On reflection, he remembered the old Archdruid had mentioned a hospital appointment in his last message.

"Oh Lord! Perhaps the old fellow is very ill and they've kept him in. I can't bother him in that state of health." Now he had thought of it, Albert felt rather guilty.

Over his second cup of tea he had a brainwave. He may not be able to rise and fall with the levitation, but could he propel himself along while he was suspended above the linoleum? Leaving his tea to go cold, he ran up the stairs to his practise room and sat into the lotus position.

After minutes of concentrating on weightlessness, he felt his bottom leave the floor. He pushed hard against the wall and felt the air in the room blow gently against his face, as he moved across the room like a hovercraft. Immediately he felt the movement he became so excited, he forgot to concentrate. The trainee druid fell with a gentle bump to the floor.

"Damn! I stopped visualising too soon!" Albert knew exactly where he had gone wrong. He knew his excitement at being able to use his new skill to propel himself along, had broken his concentration. He tried again; this time he was determined to ignore any distractions and stay weightless. It worked! His body rose half an inch above the floor, he pushed his hands firmly against the wall and sailed effortlessly across to the opposite side of the room until he felt his back bump gently against the other wall. He grinned broadly and predictably fell the to the floor.

"My God! No wonder the Wise One couldn't keep airborne when he spotted that topless usherette! It didn't take much to bring me down to earth again. The sight of a pair of double D's would bring a helicopter down!"

Albert was a resourceful old man. In the back of his mind he was forming a plan. He knew he ought to levitate up and over the barbed wire perimeter fence, but he couldn't wait for that to happen, as the Gryphon needed his help urgently. He packed his gear in a bag and drove down to Beggars Bush wood to put his plan into action.

At the woods, he changed into his towelling robe and tried the sacrificial ceremony, just in case the beast had managed to free itself. He was not at all surprised when he drew another blank.

"Right, part two of my plan." He muttered to himself as he approached the wire fence. Albert grabbed the wire mesh, closed his eyes, and directed his thought waves to the beast. Within five minutes he heard the answering cry of some large bird. That was all the confirmation he needed.

"Right my beauty. I am coming to get you!"

Albert was no youngster but he had worked on the land all his life. In retirement, he managed his woods actively and kept himself remarkably fit for his age. He checked on the trees nearest to the wire fence, which had substantial branches overlooking the barrier, searching for one projecting above the height of the coils of razor wire. Of course, none of the trees were near the wire; the security people at the plant had insisted on felling all the trees close to the fence to prevent protestors jumping over.

Albert found a suitable oak, shinned up it and sat astride a large lateral branch that projected from the trunk above the height of the perimeter fence. He managed to find a wide enough space to sit in the lotus position with his back against the tree trunk. Then he concentrated on weightlessness.

Half an hour later, Albert was still trying to rise above the tree branch, but he was finding it difficult to concentrate in such precarious surroundings. He started to get cramp in his legs and the rough bark was causing pins and needles in his bottom. The old man began to despair of ever getting airborne; the more he looked down at the ground, the more he felt his confidence slip away.

Suddenly, from the brick building immediately in front of him, he heard that strange screeching cry again. Putting all personal discomfort out of his mind, he tried one last time to rise above the tree branch.

With that encouragement, it worked! The thought of letting the Gryphon down was enough to strongly focus his thoughts. He felt his legs and bottom leave the rough tree bark until he was hovering a few inches above the branch. He rose like a traveller on an invisible magic carpet. Without opening his eyes he pushed his hands hard against the tree trunk and felt himself move through the air towards the barbed-wire fence.

After a few seconds the impetus of that single push, ran out. Albert came to a standstill somewhere in the air over the fence. The druid opened his eyes slowly and peered down at the ground. He was thrilled to see he was hovering just past the barbed-wire barrier. He knew he was a few feet inside the research compound!

"I've done it!" He raised his fist and shouted. That rash action was more than enough to break his concentration. He plummeted to the grass, snagging the hem of his gown on the razor wire as he fell.

Albert might well have hurt himself more but his dressing gown had held him up before it ripped apart and he was fortunate to land on his feet. He hit the soft ground with a bang and rolled onto the grass, knocking all the air out of his lungs.

As soon as the intruder hit the ground, the security guards sprang into action. They had noticed the old man in the woods when he had first approached the wire fence. The head of security was called to the scene and Albert was kept under constant surveillance with the security cameras. The guards watched him climb the tree and were astounded when he appeared to jump an unbelievable forty feet from the tree and over the protective fence.

"My God! Whoever he is he must be fit. He must be a trained agent or an Olympic athlete, to have such prowess!" The head of security took no chances. He despatched ten of his strongest guards to overpower this super-fit intruder.

Albert didn't know what hit him. While he still lay winded on the ground, a bag was pushed over his head, his hands were handcuffed behind his back, and he was dragged into building 37 by the posse of burly guards.

Chapter Twenty Four

Dr Steinn spent his morning trying to persuade the disembodied brain of his Uncle Enrico to communicate freely with him and share the unique knowledge it contained about the methods of creating hybrids.

'No way, nephew, no Gryphon!' Enrico was adamant. 'No body, no talk.' That was the sum total of information Dr Steinn could induce the brain to transmit to his laptop.

The doctor buried his head in his hands. This was stalemate. But he had an even more pressing problem, which he had not dare share with the brain, even though it would be drastically affected by it. How could he tell the Professor he was deteriorating, slowly but surely, in the artificial environment that had been created for him? The Ringers solution would work for a short time but the professor's brain probably had only a few weeks of useful existence left to it. The doctor could see his lifetime's ambition slipping away. It was at this critical moment in his disappointing morning, the security guards insisted on speaking to him.

He answered the urgent buzzing of his pager only after it had repeated three times. Finally, he went to the internal phone and shouted his frustrations down the telephone line.

"What the hell do you want? I left instructions that I was not, repeat NOT, to be disturbed!"

The head of security temporarily lost his nerve and spluttered a string of meaningless phrases down the line. "Well yes… We aren't disturbing you, sir… Well no…"

"Spit it out man! Now I have stopped my work and come to the phone, you might as well tell me. What do you want?"

The security chief dropped the receiver, as if it was red hot. It swung on its cord like a clock pendulum.

All eyes focused on the chief. He was the condemned man about to drink poison. No one moved to help him. The telephone receiver came to rest against the brick wall, where it hung on its twisted cord, still and lifeless. Dr Steinn's irate voice could be heard coming from it, getting louder and louder by the second.

For every crisis there is a hero. Smiffy stepped through the crowd, picked up the phone in a matter of fact way and spoke to his boss.

"Its Smiffy, Doctor Steinn. The security guards have caught an intruder who has broken through the fence. It's the old chap they saw sizing up the wire only the other day."

"Well? Why can't security deal with it?"

"They think he may be an enemy agent or something. Though he don't look like no James Bond to me!"

The phone went silent. Steinn considered the options in his mind. Maybe a break from the brain would be a good thing at this point in time. Perhaps he was getting too close to the problem. He decided to leave the sterile lab and investigate the break-in.

"Good man, Smith. I'm coming out to see for myself."

Everybody heard the doctor's reply. A sigh of relief travelled through the ranks of security guards. The chief slapped Smiffy on the back and pumped his hand with a grateful handshake. "Good man. If you ever want promotion to security, just you let me know."

Armstrong pursed his lips and glared down at this boots. Smiffy was definitely getting above himself.

Dr Steinn, still gowned and masked, let himself through the security door into the main area of building 37. The chief of security led him to the cage where they had imprisoned Albert.

Steinn pushed the cage door, expecting it to be open so that he could go in and question the old man. He turned to the chief. "Open the door, man. He looks like a helpless pensioner to me. Surely you're not afraid of him trussed up in handcuffs and blindfolded?"

"You didn't see him jump over the fifteen foot fence."

Steinn looked at the speaker in disbelief. "He jumped over the fence?"

"Yes." The chief was emphatic. "And it took ten men to subdue him."

Steinn scratched his head and shrugged his shoulders. He could hardly square this account with the evidence of his own eyes, but discretion won.

"Right. I'll question him through the bars...Can you hear me old man?"

Albert had been lying on the straw covering of his prison floor, slowly recovering his breath. He realised his hands were tied, and he could see nothing thanks to a blindfold. Steinn's question alerted him to the fact that he was the centre of attention again.

"Let me out!" He shouted. "I was only looking for the Gryphon. It's trapped in your yard somewhere and probably needs my help."

Doctor Steinn couldn't believe his ears! He had heard that voice before. He realised it was Albert Williams, the man who had sold him the land for the research plant, but more to the point, the man who had photographed the Gryphon!

No wonder the intruder knew about the Gryphon! This was worse than he had ever imagined. He turned on his security chief, narrowed his eyes and hissed accusingly.

"How the hell has this man found out so much?"

No one answered. Armstrong suspected he knew exactly what had happened, because he and his under keeper knew the beast had flown. He glared at Smiffy from under his knitted brow, daring him to speak, on pain of death!

Dr Steinn stuck his chin in the air and looked challengingly around the assembled staff. Someone among them could well be the prisoner's accomplice. Not one of them dared to meet his gaze.

"What about you, Smith? You usually have a lot to say."

Smiffy shuffled nervously on the spot and shook his head. Even he realised the dangers.

The doctor stood deep in thought, apparently oblivious to the tense crowd surrounding him. He went over the events of the morning in his mind. Finally, he shook his head in disbelief.

"You'd better all get back to your posts. I will have to think what to do with our intruder. Leave him to me." He watched in silence as the crowd melted away. They moved swiftly before he could change his mind. The security staff left the building and the animal keepers found themselves urgent work to do in the farthest corner.

Steinn leaned against the bars of Albert's cage and eyed the old man thoughtfully. What was it about old men? The professor was thwarting his plans, demanding his body back. This old chap had penetrated their defences and found out far too much about their experiments. I wish I could put them both in a bag and drown them in the caustic tank. The thought struck him then, I could kill two birds with one stone.

"Would you like a coffee, sir?" Armstrong's wheedling voice broke into his thoughts. The head keeper was desperately trying to redress the balance of power between himself and Smiffy.

Steinn looked up from his reverie and smiled wearily. "Good idea, Headstrong." He left the cage and walked over to Armstrong's desk, where he joined the two keepers at morning coffee.

"I can't belief that old man jumped the fence." Smiffy hadn't meant to voice his private thoughts, but it just came out. He looked terribly embarrassed when he realised Dr Steinn had heard him. Instead of shutting up he let his tongue run away with him. He babbled on nervously. "I wasn't doubting security...honestly, sir. It's just that he looks an old man. Too feeble to do that...Why, he must be as old as your uncle, the professor..."

Dr Steinn slammed his coffee cup on the desk and turned on the under keeper.

Smiffy backed away in terror. "I...I...didn't mean any harm, sir!"

Armstrong let his mug slip through his fingers. He stood open mouthed as he watched Steinn envelope Smiffy in his arms and kiss him!

"You're a genius, man!" The doctor was ecstatic.

Both keepers were rooted to the spot. Steinn had surely finally lost his marbles!

The doctor walked to the security door, a broad smile on his face. He could indeed kill two birds with one stone. He realised he could get rid of the agent who had found out about the Gryphon by removing his brain and freezing his body in the liquid nitrogen. Then he would be in a position to make a promise to the brain that it would have its body back. If he could only kid the professor the intruder's frozen body was his own, Enrico would spill the beans about how he had created the Gryphon.

Chapter Twenty Five

Tony called at his Uncle's house on his way home from school; he had promised he would call on Albert to see the progress the old chap had made in his druid studies. Tony wasn't really bothered about checking on his Uncle's achievements in his new religion, but he was worried about Albert's well being. The old fellow hadn't been his usual self lately. He had not been down to the Duck and Dumplings for his usual drink, nor had he been seen about the town. Tony knocked hard on the front door and waited to be admitted.

Ten minutes passed and Tony was still waiting on the step. He peered through the side window and shouted through the letterbox. There was no response, no sign of life anywhere. Tony was about to leave to try the pub, hoping his uncle had gone down for an early drink, when he noticed a full pint of milk standing at the side door. It must have been there since the early morning delivery. That discovery really bothered him.

"Where the devil does he keep that spare key?" Tony muttered under his breath. He knew there was one hidden somewhere, because the old man had mentioned it to him in the past. He turned up the plant pots, checked under the doormat and looked under the milk bottle holder, but he found no keys in any of the usual places.

"The shed! I do remember he once mentioned the shed." Tony muttered to himself as he tried to recall past conversations with Albert. Unfortunately, the shed door was jammed shut. Something had fallen down behind it and was preventing it opening. Tony put his shoulder to the door and pushed hard. He managed to force it open a small amount. Pushing his arm around the door he felt for what was obstructing it.

"Damn that hose pipe!" Tony could feel the rubber coils jammed under the shed door. After a lot of swearing and hard work, he managed to open the shed door just enough to let his arm squeeze inside. He felt around and checked the obvious hiding place. Feeling along the ledge above the door, he put his fingers on a door key covered in cobwebs.

"Hm! I only hope this one fits." The key looked as if it had been abandoned there years ago. Luckily, with a little persuasion, it did open the side door.

Tony walked through the house and picked up the post from the hall floor. It looked as if his uncle had been out all day. He put the letters on the kitchen table and went upstairs to check the bedrooms, just in case the old chap was ill in his bed. A few minutes later Tony returned to the kitchen and sat down at the table to consider his options. He had found the bed tidily made, and the bathroom neat and clean. In the kitchen, he noticed the breakfast dishes had been washed up and put away. It looked as if his uncle had gone out early that morning and had not yet returned.

"But he knew I was calling." Tony spoke aloud to the empty kitchen. His only answer was the irregular tick of the Seth Thomas mantle clock on the shelf. He checked his watch, knowing that old American shelf clock was a doubtful timekeeper.

"Five o'clock, and he's not home. Nothing keeps him out all day like that, now he's retired." But on reflection, Tony realised that something did occasionally keep the old chap out all day, and that was usually his beloved woods. He jumped up from the table and checked the hall stand where Albert hung his outdoor clothes and his druid's costume. Albert's jacket and his towelling dressing gown were nowhere to be seen.

He's gone to his woods. I'll be bound." Tony shrugged his shoulders and decided to go home for his evening meal, assuming that Albert must have got involved in one of his ceremonies and forgotten the time and their meeting.

After tea at home, which Tony ate alone, he tried to telephone his uncle to check on him and explain how they had missed each other when he called. He let the phone ring for several minutes but there was no reply. Tony checked the time and was surprised to find it was already seven o'clock.

Maybe he's in the pub, now, Tony thought. He needed little excuse to go down to the Duck and Dumplings for a pint.

"Has Albert been in?" Tony checked with Paddy.

"No. I've not seen him today. Is he alright?" Paddy seemed genuinely concerned at the old man's absence, which added to Tony's own feelings of unease. The barman's question settled matters for the young teacher. He downed his pint quickly and left for his uncle's house.

At Albert's place, Tony found everything exactly as he had left it. The milk stood on the table; the letters lay unopened.

"Right that settles it. I'm going to Beggars Bush Woods to check if he's there." Tony wasted no more time. He sprinted home, jumped in his car and drove out to the woods.

At Beggars Bush Woods, Tony was relieved to see his uncle's truck parked by the gateway. The daylight was beginning to fade as the evening drew in. Tony vaulted the gate and jogged along the woodland path to the oak grove. At the grove he found signs of recent activity. Bits of the sacrificial meat were still on the altar. He leaned over and checked its freshness. It was drying out but it must have been left there earlier that day.

"Albert. Albert!" Tony cupped his hands and shouted for his uncle. The only answer was the alarm cry of a blackbird and the distant croak of a pheasant, disturbed from its roost. Tony went back to the altar stone and checked the grass for tracks or signs. He could see where Albert had knelt down and he could trace tracks in the long grass leading towards a large oak tree, close by the perimeter fence of the Steinn plant. Tony was puzzled. Obviously Albert had been in the woods that day; his truck was still there, but there was no sign of the old chap. If he had collapsed or tripped over and injured himself so that he couldn't move, his body would have been easy to see in the white towelling robe, even in the fading light.

"Come on Albert. Where the hell are you?" Tony shouted. He stood at the base of the oak tree and looked all around him, hoping to spot some clue to Albert's whereabouts. His eyes followed the line of the perimeter fence. That was when he spotted a strip of white material fluttering in the breeze.

Tony walked over to the wire fence and stared up at the telltale piece of cloth. When he got nearer it was obvious it was towelling. He felt instinctively it was from his uncle's robe, but what was it doing fifteen feet in the air, caught on a coil of razor wire, and inside the chemical plant?

"Oh no, Albert! You haven't climbed over into there! I don't believe it...No! Even you wouldn't be that daft!" Tony dismissed the idea for the impossible notion it was, shook his head in bewilderment and started to walk back towards the road. He had gone only a few paces when he heard a car engine start up and a vehicle drive away quickly. He didn't give it another thought, until he reached the road, then he realised it was Albert's truck that he had heard.

"Damn me! He must have used another track in the woods and we missed each other." Tony was mad he had missed Albert, but relieved that his uncle was about. If the old fellow was well enough to drive home, everything must be alright.

Back in town, Tony was in for another surprise. As he skirted the empty market place in his Sierra, he noticed Albert's truck was parked there. That was nowhere near his uncle's house or the Duck and Dumplings. Tony screeched to a halt, jumped out of the Sierra, and went over to the parked vehicle. There he found yet another mystery. The bonnet of the truck was still very warm and the exhaust was ticking as it contracted. The passenger door was partly open and the key was swinging in the ignition.

"Hell! What is the old chap up to?" Tony stood in the market square and looked around him. There was no sign of his uncle or any other driver. The only sign of life at that time of night was the off licence on the corner, but a quick glance confirmed it was empty of customers.

This is getting to be a Sherlock Holmes, one pipe mystery, Tony thought, completely baffled by it all. He decided to remove the keys from the truck and lock the doors, then he walked slowly back to his car and waited.

Twenty minutes later, he was still sitting in his car watching over the parked truck. There had been no sign of his uncle and he was getting more and more worried. Finally he made up his mind to wait no longer. He started up the Sierra, hesitated for a few more minutes willing the old chap to appear from somewhere, then drove to Albert's house for one last look.

The house was in total darkness. It was not what Tony had hoped for but it was what he'd half expected. He walked around to the back door and noticed a note pinned to the milk basket on the doorstep. That was new. He knew that note wasn't there when he had taken in the day's milk. His uncle must have been home to write that note. But where was the old chap now?

Tony walked all around the property once more, peering in at the windows and rattling the letterbox. Things were not right, he felt it in his bones. On impulse he unfolded the note left for the milkman.

'Milk is cancelled until further notice. Gone away for a holiday.'

"Gone away for a holiday? Never!" Tony took the piece of paper to his car and checked the writing. One glance in a good light and he knew it wasn't Albert's usual scrawl. This note was a fake! Albert was not due to go away on holiday and he hadn't written to the milkman. Things were getting out of hand. He was mystified. Reluctantly he knew he'd have to call on his mother and tell her, her brother had disappeared!

Freda Tompkins did not see her brother's absence as anything sinister. "What are you thinking about, Tony? You'll be telling me next the Mafia have kidnapped him!" She wagged her finger disapprovingly at her son. "I'll have to get him a good wife. He needs looking after."

Tony shook his head in disbelief. Getting Albert married off seemed the only thing his mother was worried about. He left her plotting Albert's wedding and went home.

Tony let himself into his house and went straight up to his room. He was genuinely worried about Albert's disappearance but unsure what to do next. He lay on his back on his bed, put his hands behind his head and stared at the ceiling, while he went through all he had discovered.

It must have been ten minutes later, Tony realised he could hear voices coming from the adjoining bedroom. Diana Scullery had come home and she must be in there. But, who the hell was she talking to? Albert's problems were driven straight out of his mind as he considered what was happening next door. He stepped into his wardrobe, stepping on the clothes strewn all over the bottom of it. Taking great care not to close the door behind him, he lined his eye up with the spy hole.

At first Tony couldn't see anything, then realised the back of someone's head was leaning against the other end of his lens, completely obscuring his view.

"Damn!" Tony whispered his frustration. He placed his ear against the spy hole and listened intently.

"I'm sure the Gryphon is one of their illegal experiments." Diana seemed concerned. It showed in her voice.

"I must get in to confirm it, but they are very tight on security." It was a deeper, male voice.

Tony frowned. Diana had a man in her room. Who the hell was it?

"Then there's that photograph of the cryogenic tank. What would an ordinary biological research lab want with one of those?"

Tony thumped his fist into his hand as he recognised the voice. It was Reynard Muldoon. That ruddy PE teacher again! He was obviously making out with Diana. Damn him! He'd already wheedled his way into her bedroom! Tony pressed his eye closer to the lens.

The teachers in the next room seemed to be discussing something very seriously. They moved about the room, sometimes coming into Tony's field of view and at other times being completely out of sight. He watched with a growing feeling of bewilderment as they sat on the bed together and just talked. There was no familiarity. They looked for all the world as if they were holding a briefing meeting. Suddenly he heard a familiar name mentioned.

"Tony's Uncle Albert concerns me. He has made no secret of seeing the Gryphon. If they realise his involvement he might be a target for silencing." That was Diana speaking.

That settled it! Tony stumbled out of wardrobe and rushed along the corridor. He tapped on Diana's door and waited.

"Oh! Hello Tony." She opened the door only a fraction to prevent him seeing inside he room. "What can I do for you?"

Tony coloured up with embarrassment but blurted out what he had to say.

"I heard you mention my Uncle Albert just now. He's disappeared and I'm worried about him."

Diana looked shocked.

"The walls are thin and I was being very quiet...I heard you talking to Muldoon...Honest I wasn't spying on you..." Tony stumbled over his excuses.

"You'd better come in." She ushered him into the small bedroom and closed the door behind them. Tony nodded at Muldoon and looked quickly away.

"Tony tells me his uncle has vanished. He's worried." Diana exchanged a knowing look with the PE teacher.

"I know he was at the woods performing his druid ceremonies, but I couldn't find him. I saw a piece of his towelling robe caught on the top of the razor wire fence. It was on the other side! "

His listeners exchanged more puzzled glances.

"I followed his truck into town but it was parked in the market place and left with the door open. And the key swinging in the ignition. He hasn't been home but someone wrote a note cancelling his milk." He fished the folded piece of paper from his pocket.

Muldoon let out a long low whistle and turned to Diana. "Looks as if your suspicions were well founded."

"What suspicions?" Tony could contain his curiosity no longer.

"Sit down, Tony. We'd better explain." Diana gestured to the bed. When he had made himself comfortable she continued. "Rey and I work together as special agents for the government. We came here posing as teachers as our cover story. Our masters are sure that Steinn Brothers are performing unauthorised experiments on animal embryos and probably planning to clone the results. We know they have connections with an Italian group that is advanced in these experiments and we think that group is Mafia funded. The department has inspected the Runford plant officially, but nothing was found. We are here to check them out unofficially."

As she spoke, Tony's mind raced. Special agents! That explained the gun. He'd had a narrow escape; Diana was well out of his league. What if she'd found out about the spy hole? Self-consciously he glanced up at the hidden lens. When Diana completed her explanation, he shook off his own concerns and concentrated on what she had said. He was beginning to see her reasons for believing in Albert's Gryphon. All along, she had suspected a connection with the

Steinn plant and their unauthorised animal experiments.

"Experiments on animals? How come they sent two special agents for such a small thing?"

"We believe Steinn is on the threshold of combining the genes of any two species. He has a Gryphon; what about a Centaur?"

"A horse with a human trunk? Human-animal crosses!" Tony looked shocked.

"Imagine what an army of Centaurs or even winged soldiers, could achieve. Steinn has no scruples. He'd sell his expertise to the highest bidder. In any event, we can't wait for the worst scenario. He's already broken the law by experimenting with genetics without a valid license." Muldoon explained.

"How unscrupulous?" Tony queried. "Unscrupulous enough to harm an old man who stumbled on his secret by accident?"

Diana just nodded.

Chapter Twenty Six

Early next morning, Albert woke up behind bars, with a crick in his back and a stiff neck. He had hardly slept and when he did eventually nod off in the early hours of the morning from sheer exhaustion, the handcuffs biting into his wrists and the blindfold around his eyes, made it impossible for him to relax for long.

He opened his eyes in a panic. He'd been dreaming he'd been fighting in a war and he'd been taken prisoner and thrown into a dungeon. He found the reality was worse than his nightmare. He did indeed seem to be locked in some kind of a cell!

Memories of the previous day flooded back to Albert. He had gone over the wire fence and he had trespassed onto the Steinn Brother's property, but he didn't deserve to be thrown in gaol. Those security men had overreacted in a big way.

When I get out I'll sue them! In that militant frame of mind he started to shout for attention, intending to demand his release, but no one came to see what he wanted. After a few minutes of fruitless yelling he calmed down and took stock of his situation, realising it could be early in the morning and long before any of the staff were at work. In the silence of the early hours he nodded off to sleep again.

Smiffy was first in to building 37 that morning. Armstrong had permission to come in later as he had a dental appointment. The under keeper fed all the animals in the building, including the Gryphon, then went to check on the prisoner, who was still fast asleep. Smiffy felt extremely sorry for the old man and decided to prepare breakfast for him. Dr Steinn had given instructions that Albert was to be kept as fit as possible, so Smiffy had brought in some cereal and two extra pints of milk. He boiled the milk and took the food to the cage.

"Morning. Time for your breakfast." Smiffy tried to sound cheerful.

Albert, who was still blindfold and handcuffed, didn't answer.

"You in there. I've made breakfast for you. You do eat cereals, don't you?"

Albert roused himself, realised the voice was addressing him and sat up in the straw, stretching his aching arms out behind him. "How the devil can I eat trussed up like this!"

Smiffy considered the problem. The prisoner had a point. Surely there was no harm in taking off the old fellows blindfold and unlocking his handcuffs? After all, he was still locked up in a cage. What harm could he do in there? If the doctor wanted the prisoner kept fit, he had to be allowed to eat properly.

"Come over here to the bars. I will undo your blindfold and take off those cuffs, but you'd better behave if you want any breakfast."

Albert nodded agreement. There was little he could do, with his hands numb from the long imprisonment in handcuffs. He made his way towards the voice.

Smiffy undid the cuffs and removed the blindfold through the gap in the bars. Then he placed the cereal bowl and a spoon on the floor next to the prisoner. Before departing, he checked that the door was still securely locked.

Albert recovered slowly. It took several minutes for his eyes to get used to the daylight and for any feeling to return to his fingers. Gradually his vision cleared, the tingling stopped in his hands and he managed to eat his breakfast.

"Is there any more." He shouted to Smiffy, trying to get the keeper to come back to talk to him.

"You can have the same again, if you like. I suppose you must be hungry with no supper last night." He prepared another bowl of cereal and pushed it through the bars of the cage.

"Can't you let me out?" Albert pleaded.

"No. It's more than my life's worth. Dr Steinn would have my guts for garters if you escaped. Anyway, as a secret agent, you know the rules; you must have seen them James Bond films."

Albert looked at Smiffy in amazement. Secret agent? What was the idiot on about? "I'm no secret agent. I'm just an ordinary pensioner."

"Ah well! You would say that, wouldn't you. What about leaping over a fifteen feet high barbed wire fence? That don't sound like the action of no ordinary pensioner to me."

Albert was on the point of explaining about levitation but decided against it, realising how unlikely the truth would sound. Somehow these people had the wrong idea about him. He decided to keep quiet and behave himself, in the hope they would realise he was no threat to them. Then he hoped they would eventually let him go. Maybe when this doctor turned up for work he could explain things to him. In the meantime, he would pass his time by concentrating on his studies.

Mid morning, when Armstrong appeared for work, the head of security decided that Albert should be hidden from the sight of anyone who happened to visit the animal cages. The less people knew about their prisoner, the better. He ordered Smiffy and Armstrong to erect a screen of tarpaulins in front of the cage, completely blocking the view. Now Albert could not see what was going on in the building, but neither could he be easily observed.

In the peace of his cage, Albert tried practising his telepathy. He was still curious about the Gryphon and tried to make contact with the beast, as he had in the woods. It took him several minutes to get a response, but when he did make contact he was thrilled to hear the beast was only a short distance away from him. The answering shriek came from another part of the same building! They must have imprisoned the Gryphon as they had imprisoned him!

"Shut up!" Armstrong yelled at the beast. "Stop that shrieking!"

"I'll go and see what's wrong with it." Smiffy volunteered.

Albert heard the responses and listened attentively to the under keeper's conversation.

"Nothing wrong. I stroked it and soothed it down. Maybe its all these goings on that's upset it. Not surprising really. I'm not happy myself about keeping that old chap under lock and key."

"Well we can't let him go. Dr Steinn said he had a use for him." Armstrong explained.

Albert didn't like the sound of that. If they thought he was spying, and had taken the law into their own hands by locking him up, there was no telling when they would let him go. What they had done already was against the law. He decided to try and contact the outside world by telepathy. If he could reach out and let someone know where he was, there was a chance he'd get out. He sat cross legged on the straw strewn floor of his cage and concentrated on making contact with the old Archdruid, realising he was the only person with the skill to receive the distress signal.

The animal keepers went about their daily routine. Security looked in to check that they had screened off the prisoner. Time passed slowly. Albert sat cross legged on the straw and tried his hardest to make mental contact with his teacher. He was pleased in some ways that the keepers couldn't see what he was doing. They wouldn't have really known what he was up to, as he sat deep in concentration, but with no interruptions he could concentrate better.

Albert sent out his SOS for ten minutes then stilled his mind for a similar period, to detect any answering call. This process he repeated all through the morning.

"Help! Help! Come on Archdruid." He muttered in frustration. "Please make contact. You're my only hope." Then he let his mind go blank ready to receive the reply. Suddenly some strange thoughts entered his head. The speech pattern was definitely not that of Arthur Cobbold, the Wiseone he was used to contacting! Maybe he's still in hospital and the drugs are affecting him? Albert thought. Then the voice in his head became clearer.

'Who is this? ' There was no mistaking the words or the foreign accent.

'Are you foreign?' Albert formed the thought.

'No. I'm Italian. You sound foreign!'

That reply made Albert stop and think. If he had managed to contact someone in Italy he would have a problem getting them to understand the urgency of his situation. He tried again.

'Where are you?'

'I'm in the Steinn Brothers laboratory in England.'

"Good God!" Albert exclaimed aloud, forgetting himself and breaking into proper speech. If someone in the Steinn Brother's plant was getting his messages, he was found out! They'd be along any minute to stop him! He panicked.

'What's the matter?' The Italian voice sounded in his head.

'Nothing, nothing at all.' Albert tried to hide his true thoughts, but it was impossible in his state of panic.

'Don't worry about Dr Steinn. I have nothing to thank my nephew for either.'

'Nephew? Who are you?'

'I am Professor Enrico Steinn, Dr Frank Steinn's uncle. He has me imprisoned in a laboratory and he's keeping me out of my body!'

Albert couldn't believe he'd heard properly.

'Out of your...er... body?'

'Yes. I am a disembodied brain, kept alive in the laboratory. My body is preserved in liquid nitrogen. I actually died, but he wouldn't let me rest. The man is a menace!'

Albert paced up and down his prison like a caged bear with bad psychological problems. The situation was much worse than he had imagined. Dr Steinn kept brains in a tank and bodies in nitrogen. The man must be mad! He tried to keep his thought to himself and cut out the voice in his head. He had to think this situation out without being overheard by anyone.

At mid day, Smiffy pulled the tarpaulin curtain aside and brought the prisoner his lunch.

"We sent out for fish and chips. I hope that suits you? They are still hot." He tried to keep cheerful when he spoke to Albert.

"That's fine." Albert was feeling hungry. "But when am I going to be let out?"

Smiffy ignored the question. He wasn't sure what Dr Steinn had in mind for the prisoner, but it was more than his life was worth to get involved.

"I shall be missed, you know. My family live in Runford and I visit them every day. You'll have the police here in no time." Albert tried to sound positive when he threatened.

Smiffy shrugged his shoulders. He could see trouble coming but he daren't do anything that would upset the doctor. Once he had left the cage he grumbled to his boss.

"I don't like this at all. It's not legal to imprison pensioners like this. There's going to be trouble over this, you mark my words."

Armstrong shook his head helplessly. He knew Smiffy was right but he was even more petrified of their boss.

Albert wasn't sure what to do now that someone else had made contact with him. Unfortunately, that someone was related to the Steinn brothers. He decided it would be safer if he kept himself busy by practising his levitation, and left the mental telepathy well alone.

The cage that security had used to imprison Albert was extremely high. It had vertical iron bars at the front and the other three walls were brick, with no windows or other openings in them. When he looked up to check the height of the walls, he could see they stretched right up to the roof of the building. There was a large square skylight let into the roof above his head. It had a translucent plastic centre that let in some diffused daylight. Albert glanced up at the brickwork and estimated the ceiling was at least thirty feet above him. If only I could levitate properly and not just raise my bottom a few inches from the ground, he thought angrily, maybe I could get out onto that roof and make my escape.

Albert concentrated on his levitation exercises with renewed vigour and ignored the mental messages he kept receiving from Professor Steinn, hoping the professor would get fed up with getting no replies and stop pestering him.

At about two o'clock in the afternoon, the tarpaulin curtain was pulled back. Two men stood looking at Albert through the bars. He had been concentrating on his exercises and had only just heard the visitors in time. He stopped concentrating and returned to earth with a bump. Judging by the impact he felt on his backside, he had managed to rise at least a foot above the straw strewn floor. He looked up and saw from their name badges it was a Doctor F Steinn and the Head of Security staring at him.

The security chief only stayed a few minutes. He had come to check that his orders were being carried out correctly. When he was satisfied that the prisoner was being fed and watered and there was no chance of him escaping, he took leave of his boss and went back to his office. Steinn stood alone and stared at Albert. He nodded to himself as if he was satisfied about something, then eyed Albert curiously, obviously deep in thought.

Albert returned the stare, wondering exactly what the doctor was thinking. He decided to try and tune into the man's mind.

'Well Albert Williams, you're about the right height and weight. About the right age. I couldn't have found a better fit, if I'd advertised in a dating agency!'

Albert coloured up. Surely the man wasn't fancying a date with him? He scowled then made himself relax, realising his own thoughts would be showing on his face.

'He looks healthy enough. The security chief says he can jump over a fifteen foot fence. I can't really believe that. I think the chief is making excuses to cover up his own incompetence. This old chap will do nicely to house the professor's brain. Yes. Fate has provided me with the perfect recipient.' Dr Steinn nodded at Albert, smiled secretively, and walked away, letting the canvas curtain close behind him.

Left alone, Albert pondered on what he had just learned. The facts all fitted in with what the strange voice had said. There obviously was a professor and he was just a brain. Dr Steinn needed a new body for the brain, so something had happened to the professor's original body. Albert considered this dispassionately until he realised the implications for his own body!

"Hell! I'm to supply the new body!" He spoke out loud.

"You alright?" Smiffy asked. The keeper had been hovering in the background as Dr Steinn and the security chief eyed up the old man. Although he was reluctant to do anything about the prisoner, Smiffy was feeling more and more guilty. He parted the tarpaulin screen and asked again. "You alright, in there?"

Albert stood up and smiled at the keeper. "I'm fine, but what happened to the professor's body?"

Smiffy stepped back, stunned by the question. No one but the doctor and he knew anything about the body in the caustic tank. Smiffy thought fast.

'God! If the prisoner knows and Frank Steinn finds out the prisoner knows, I'm a dead man!'

"I wouldn't wish you dead. I wont tell him, if you don't." Albert answered aloud.

Smiffy gulped. "How…how…how did you…do that?"

"I read minds." Albert was matter of fact about his ability. "You've told me so much already with your thoughts. Why not tell me where the professor's body is now."

"It's...it's.. in the caustic tank. Completely dissolved by now."

Albert scratched the back of his head. It was obvious the professor's brain didn't know about this. It was still talking about rejoining its body at some future date. He would have to be careful how he handled this knowledge.

"How long can the brain live out of its body?" Albert asked Smiffy."I'm no scientist, but from what I've heard Dr Steinn saying, it can't last long."

Albert sat down on his straw floor covering and considered his options. He now knew if he hung about for long he would be just become a spare part for Steinn's experiments! He threw caution to the wind and tried again with all his might, to contact the Wise One in Macclesfield.

Chapter Twenty Seven

Tony was beside himself with worry. What he had learned from Diana and Rey was enough to upset anyone. He toyed with the idea of telling his mother, but he couldn't see what good that would do. Why worry her unnecessarily? He called at the police station on his way to school the next morning.

"Yes sir?" The constable on the desk seemed affable enough.

"I want to report a missing person. Possibly a kidnapping."

The policeman raised his eyebrows.

"My uncle is missing."

"How long has he been missing, sir?"

"Two days. And he left a note."

"Ah! Let's see the note."

Tony handed the piece of paper over.

"Well, there you are. He's gone on holiday. He says so here. I wouldn't worry sir. He'll be back in a week or so."

"But you don't understand. That's not his writing."

"Oh! Well maybe he got a friend to write it. Does he have difficulty writing? Do I know your uncle, sir?"

"Albert Williams. You may remember him sitting in the market place dressed as a Buddhist monk."

"Ah! I see sir. We all remember him! Look son, I'm sure your uncle has a perfectly good reason to be absent. Maybe he's gone to Tibet or somewhere. Maybe the Dalai Lama has invited him over for the weekend." The constable screwed up the missing persons' form he had started to prepare, and threw it into the waste bin.

Tony could see he was not being taken seriously. He left the police station in a very disgruntled mood and decided he would contact Diana Scullery and Reynard Muldoon at school. By first break, Tony was feeling unusually worried about Uncle Albert. For some vague reason he could not fathom, images of the old man locked in a cage, kept popping into his mind. It was irrational, he knew, but he couldn't shake off the feeling that Albert was trying to tell him something, and that time was fast running out. He let his class out a few minutes before the bell, and rushed down to the Biology lab.

"Diana. I'm worried. I keep getting this awful feeling that Albert is in dire trouble. I think his life is in danger. I know it's irrational, but we are close and he can read my mind at times." Tony blurted out. Several students overheard what he said. They stood at their benches, all flapping ears and open mouths at his comments.

Diana ushered him quickly into the privacy of the preparation room off the main laboratory, and made her class file out into the corridor.

She returned to Tony and told him. "Reynard is coming over any minute now. We had arranged to talk this over at first break, when we had both had a chance to think about it."

Tony nodded glumly. Then he cheered up. At least Diana was taking his fears seriously. The Runford police had been no help at all. He thanked her. "Thanks for that vote of confidence, Diana. The police just weren't interested."

Diana frowned. "I have my doubts about the Runford police. Steinn is very friendly with the Chief Constable and with the local Inspector. He's made generous donations to the Police Benevolent Fund. The three of them play golf together and they seem to be bosom buddies."

Tony's mouth dropped open and his eyes widened in disbelief.

"You may well look shocked, Tony. Steinn has several MP's in his pocket apart from the ones on his board of directors. Brown paper envelopes stuffed with used fifty pound notes can buy lots of friends in high places."

Tony drew in a sharp intake of breath and was about to ask her to name names when they were interrupted.

"Sorry I'm late." Rey ran into the laboratory. "The lower sixth are so slow. I wish I'd got them in the army for a week!"

"Tony's been getting strong feelings of impending danger. He thinks they come from his uncle. I don't usually hold with this X-files nonsense, but this time I'm inclined to agree with him. If Albert managed to break into the Steinn plant he should have been thrown out long ago. If they're keeping him there, he must have seen something they don't want the outside world to know about."

Rey nodded as he munched hungrily on a chocolate bar.

"We must get into the plant and find out what's happening." Diana looked pointedly at the PE teacher. "You are the muscle in this partnership. What do you suggest?"

"I'll go in tonight. I'll have to cut the fence and get in from the woods. But I'll need a diversion to buy some time. They'll be on high alert and they'll have the entire fence covered by their security cameras."

Tony had listened to this conversation in silence. Suddenly he had a brainwave.

"I'll create a diversion if you like. If I get the animal rights protestors to storm the front gates, that will keep their security staff more than busy."

"Good man." Rey slapped him on the back, nearly knocking him over. Turning to Diana he asked. "Is that OK with you? As senior officer you must have the last say."

"Just don't get caught, Rey. They will be armed, I'm sure. And we don't want any publicity about government agents breaking into places."

After break, Tony was scheduled for a free period to catch up on his marking. He took the opportunity to locate the sixth form history group, who were studying in the library. He took Dickinson to one side and asked for his help.

"I need a favour, Dickinson. Can you mobilise your animal rights friends to storm the gate at the Steinn plant?"

Dickinson's face broke into a broad smile. "You going to support us, sir? I knew you were the sensitive type and couldn't stand by while helpless animals are butchered in the name of science."

Tony smiled wanly, and nodded doubtful agreement. He could hardly explain the real reason for his request. Hastily, he outlined his fake reasons.

"It's this evening we must demonstrate. We need to create a diversion Sorry. I mean we ought to create trouble at the main gate, this evening." He realised how weak this bald statement must have sounded, so he embroidered the story, adding some fictional details of his own invention. "I have contacts and I've heard they are planning some diabolical animal experiments on fluffy little kittens, this very evening. Get as many of your friends as you can to come. We need a big demo. Maybe you could lay your hands on some fireworks and smoke bombs to cause the maximum disturbance."

Dickinson pulled out his mobile phone and immediately started ringing his mates. This was going to be a night to remember. He had visions of his photograph in the national press and becoming a hero to all the other animal rights enthusiasts. His eyes glowed with enthusiasm. He had been asked officially to front a demonstration; this was going to shape his destiny. In his imagination the Directorship of the RSPCA beckoned.

Tony hurried from the library and ran down to the staff car park. He realised his mother had no inkling of what had happened to her brother and he daren't keep her in the dark any longer. He knew exactly where he would find her that afternoon. It was the day the WI organised their practical demonstrations at the church hall. Usually it was flower arranging or a talk on cookery, both of which Freda enjoyed, so Tony was sure she would be there.

He parked his car beside the pile of lady's bicycles at the back of the church hall, took a deep breath to steel himself for the ordeal and went inside.

"Pretend I am coming at you with a knife." A male voice bellowed out. A small wiry woman grabbed the large man by his wrist. As easily as she would have shaken a pillow, she flicked him over her back. The man thumped onto the mat on the floor, all the air knocked out of him.

Tony stood just inside the doorway until he spotted his mother.

"Mum! I want a word with you." He sauntered over to her and held out his hand.

"Ah yes!" Freda grabbed her son's extended wrist and threw him onto his back, keeping the wrist in one steely grip, she shot her other arm around his throat and applied a deadly strangle hold. Tony choked and spluttered helplessly. This was too much!

"We're having self-defence classes." Freda looked down at her crestfallen son and explained, rather unnecessarily.

"Well I'm not attacking you, am I. I'm only here because I want an urgent word with you about Uncle Albert."

"Oh yes! What's the silly old fool been up to now?"

"I think he's been kidnapped. He's not at home. He went to his woods. He's not been seen since."

"Don't fret, Tony. He's gone off on some crazy quest or other. The sooner I've got him married off to a sensible woman, the better." Freda loosened her grip on her son's throat and let him get up.

"I am not kidding, mother. I found a bit of his belt caught inside the barbed wire at the Steinn plant. He's obviously climbed over the fence. There's not hair nor hide of him in any of his usual haunts." Tony shook his head in despair and the seriousness of his message at last got through to his mother.

"You mean it, lad, don't you. Tell me all you know. We'll see what can be done."

Mother and son left the hall and sat in Tony's car where he explained all he knew about Albert's disappearance.

Freda listened in silence then got out of the Sierra.

"You get back to school, Tony. I'll think about this and I'll see you at the Steinn plant this evening." Her brow creased in thought, she returned to her self-defence class.

Tony drove back to school and his next class. He couldn't see what else he could do about Albert, but he was satisfied he had put in hand all the schemes he could think of, to free the old man. He had mobilised the animal rights brigade to create a diversion. He had alerted two government secret agents who had taken him seriously enough to want to investigate his claims. Most importantly, he had let his mother know what was happening. To leave Freda out of things would have been the biggest mistake of all. If anything happened to Uncle Albert and his sister hadn't been notified about it, Tony knew his life would not be worth living.

Chapter Twenty Eight

Runford railway station was exceptionally busy. The solitary porter on duty couldn't fathom what was happening. It was usually so quiet and sleepy.

"Beggars Bush wood is on the Fen Road. It's about two miles out of town. You can't miss it. It's next to Steinn Brothers research plant." The porter explained, for the tenth time that morning. He took off his cap and scratched the back of his head, trying to fathom what was going on.

The serious young man, who had asked for directions, bowed his shaven head in thanks, picked up his rucksack and his small leather suitcase and walked through the archway, out of the station.

"Just like all the others." The porter muttered to himself. "Must be a rock festival or something planned for Albert Williams woods. I wonder if the old fellow has agreed to it?"

The main road from the North was equally busy. At Alf's Transport Café on the roundabout at the top of the town, a young man leapt down from a lorry cab and shouted his thanks to the driver, in an unmistakable northern accent. He picked up his rucksack and ambled towards the open door of the transport café. Inside, he was greeted loudly by a dozen of his mates.

"Ee ba gum. It's our Jim!"

He raised a hand in acknowledgement and went up to the counter.

"A coffee please, and 'appen you can tell me t' way t'...?" He got no further with his request. The grizzled old man behind the counter, who was juggling three cups at once below a single steaming tap, pointed with his elbow and nodded his head towards a card, suspended above the water heater.

Jim read the message, scrawled in large red letters. 'You are here. Beggars Bush wood is here.' A crude but effective map was drawn below the words.

The lad thanked him and studied the map as he waited for his coffee.

"Here. You can a take a these a coffees over to your a mates." Alfonso the café proprietor, spoke at last, his unlikely accent a rich mixture of Lincolnshire brogue and his native Italian. During the Second World War Alfonso had been a prisoner of war in the fens. He had married a local girl and stayed there. The old chap nodded towards a table by the window, where several young men with rucksacks, were talking loudly.

"Bloody foreigners!" Alfonso, who regarded himself as a genuine Lincolnshire Yellow Belly, after his many years in the area, grumbled to his waitress. "They've a been arriving alla day. Come a downa here from the North and a make a the noise in our woods. Bloody foreigners, they are!"

The young man sat down with his friends.

"Eh up, Jim! Glad you could make it t' bash." Several of them greeted him like old friends, slapping him on the back and making room at the table for him.

The men kept arriving in dribs and drabs. It seemed a very unlikely crowd for a rock festival. There were no girls among them. They were all unusually quiet and reserved. They took great pains to avoid the entrance to the Steinn plant, and they all entered the woods at the far side. It was almost as if they did not want it to be known they were in the area. By mid morning there were at least a hundred young men dispersed through Albert's woods, their tents hidden among the trees, pitched well away from the perimeter fence of the Steinn Brothers plant. Jim unrolled his rucksack and pitched his tent under a large oak tree, beside several others.

At mid day the sound of a faint gong was heard echoing through the woodland. From their tents, an army of white clad men issued, each one attired in an outfit more or less like Albert's druid outfit. They sat on the grass, crossed legged in a circle, as they waited in silence for their leader. Finally an elderly man in a tatty white robe, stood in the middle of them. They bowed their heads to the grass and simultaneously uttered a deep 'Ohm' sound, which reverberated in their chests, echoing among the trees, silencing the birds and other wildlife. Even the constant rustle of the trees seemed to hesitate at the sound. Druid Albert Entwhistle held up his hand for their attention.

"Hail brothers. I bring greetings from t' Wise One. Unfortunately he is still in t' hospital. 'Appen he may soon be passing on to another life." The heads bowed in unison at this bad news. The leader cleared his throat and spoke again.

"I summoned you here because brother Pollawsdoc, our presumptive leader, needs us t' help."

One of the much younger druids was overcome with excitement. He punched the air with a clenched fist and shouted a strident but unintelligible rallying cry. The others looked at him askance.

"Enough of that, lad! 'T ain;'t a bloody football match you know. 'Appen many of us will be laid low before t' day's over." The old man raised a hand to his forehead, shielding his eyes as he looked over the seated crowd, searching for familiar faces.

"How many of t' Clogarte Black Belts have we among us?"

Scattered among the crowd, four hands were held aloft. Jim and the other younger acolytes looked about them in awe. They had heard about the fabulous exploits of these experts in the martial art, many had seen demonstrations, but never had they seen so many of them gathered together in one place at one time, and never had they witnessed Clogarte used in anger. Their breasts filled with pride. This was going to be a campaign to remember. An exploit to tell their grandchildren about.

"I'll brief you Black Belts in my tent after t' dinner." The old man nodded to his four experienced warriors. "T' rest of you will be told what to do after t' campaign is planned." He bowed to the crowd to dismiss them and stalked back to his tent.

Jim walked back to his own tent, talking quietly to his mates.

"'Appen we'll see some action, then? How come we've been summoned all this way down t' South to see Pollawsdoc?".

One of the lads spoke up. He seemed to be better informed than the rest of them.

"I travelled down in t' bus wit' Albert Entwhistle, he's a council member. He's been in touch wit' Wise One on his mobile. He reckons Pollawsdoc contacted t' Wise One by telepathy and he's imprisoned somewhere in that there chemical plant."

Jim raised his eyebrows in amazement. He regarded telepathy and those higher reaches of the esoteric art, well beyond him, as he was only a plumber's apprentice.

"I'd never heard of t' Pollawsdoc, before this. Had you?"

"Nay lad. It seems Pollawsdoc was directed to t' Archdruid by a higher force. It seems he has t' power to raise mythical beasts and suchlike."

"How come he needs our help to get out, then?"

"Search me! Old druid Entwhistle thinks Pollawsdoc is a natural leader in the making, but he still has a lot to learn yet. T' Old Archdruid has been teaching him by telepathy."

"Ee ba gum! That's heavy stuff. Too heavy for me! But I'm glad I'm here. I feel in my water, t' druid history will be made here."

Jim's mate eyed him warily. That bit about feeling something in his water and about history being made, sounded awfully like some kind of prophesy. He had always relied on Jim to keep his feet on t' ground. Now t' lad was predicting coming events. He was not so sure that he liked that turn of events. Maybe t' druidism was beginning to have an effect; even on t' humble plumber's mate.

After dinner, Druid Entwhistle and the Clogarte Black Belts held a council of war. Plans were made to storm the Steinn plant and look for the imprisoned Pollawsdoc."After dark. That's t' best time. Surprise is our best ally." One of the leading experts, with a tenth Dan in Clogarte addressed the group.

"I vote we send two of t' group out to reconnoitre the fence before we make solid plans." They all agreed that made sense.

"There's a lot of buildings in t' chemical plant. 'Appen Pollawsdoc could be in any one of t' em. Can we be more specific?" Another voice asked.

Druid Entwhistle held up his hand for silence. "Pollawsdoc is sending out t' telepathic 'may day' messages. T' Wise One picked t' em up in hospital. I think myself and some of t' other experienced druids should set up t' mental watch to listen out for him. 'Appen we can pin point his whereabouts then."

There was some doubt expressed about their ability to use ESP at that level. Most of the assembled druids had concentrated on the Clogarte aspect of the training, but as no better idea was forthcoming, they agreed to set up a watching and listening brief, while two of their number visited the fence to check out the layout of the Steinn Brothers site.

Chapter Twenty Nine

Inside building 37 the daily routine of feeding and cleaning out the experimental animals was going on unhindered. Smiffy and Armstrong checked on the Eagle-dog and all the other animals. They cleaned out the dogs, cats, rats, mice and rabbits giving them new bedding, changing their drinking water and removing any uneaten food. They worked together without speaking, each one absorbed in his own thoughts of what had happened to them. It was not every day they were responsible for a human prisoner and they weren't happy about it. Suddenly they were interrupted by a piercing screech.

"The hybrid seems a bit uptight today." Armstrong stood well back from the cage, leaned on his broom and pointed at the Eagle/ dog, who was crying out and pacing his cage in an agitated state. "You don't think the prisoner has anything to do with it, do you?"

Smiffy wiped his nose on his sleeve and scratched the back of his neck. "Don't see why."

Albert, who was in the far corner of his locked cage, still sitting cross legged on the straw and trying desperately to send out telepathic messages for help, ignored their conversation. He forced himself to breath slowly and evenly as he tried to project his messages into the ether.

The Eagle-dog screeched at the top of its voice, interrupting Albert's flow. The old man nodded knowingly to himself. He knew in his heart that call was from his Gryphon. They had the beast imprisoned somewhere in the building close by. If he escaped he vowed he would also release the Gryphon.

The interruptions Albert had endured from the disembodied brain had grown less and less. Gradually, Professor Enrico Steinn's thoughts had stopped getting through to him. Albert was a bit concerned about the professor because it was obvious the old man was weak and losing strength rapidly, but he knew the freedom of them all would depend on him making the outside world aware of their plight.

After he'd eaten his dinner, which Smiffy prepared with special care and pushed through the bars, Albert sat in silent contemplation, trying to make his mind receptive to any reaction to his messages. It was then, he felt a presence nearby!

"Good God!" Albert spoke quietly to himself. "I'm, sure there's a druid nearby. I definitely got the feeling that someone was trying to reach me." He closed his eyes and let his mind go vacant. Slowly a vision of leaves and trees drifted into his mind. Excitedly he realised he could see his own woods in his mind's eye, and his stone altar slab was surrounded by white coated druids. They were nearby! If only he could contact them. He redoubled his efforts to transmit a message, trying to lead them to building 37 where he was caged.

In the private laboratory where Dr Steinn had kept the brain, things were not going well. The professor's brain was failing fast. The artificial environment, Steinn had prepared for it was proving totally inadequate. The Doctor turned up the oxygen supply and checked the temperature of the bath, for the tenth time that hour.

"I must transplant Uncle's brain into a donor body very soon. It will be my last chance of extracting the information on his breakthrough." Dr Steinn was panicking. "I will have to operate on the prisoner tonight." He talked out loud to himself in the silence of the empty laboratory, trying to reassure himself he had everything under control. He rechecked the computer readings. The brain appeared to be resting but many of its vital signs were getting much too faint for comfort. Things were getting very desperate.

"I'll go and inspect the prisoner again. I'm sure he's the right age and type to be an ideal recipient." Steinn stalked out of his private laboratory and went through the security door to the main part of building 37.

Armstrong heard the security door slide open. "Eh up? We have company." He warned his underling of their boss's approach. Smiffy carried on sweeping the floor, whistling tunelessly to himself.

"How is the prisoner? He's a spy you know. I will have to let him go tonight." Steinn spoke those unlinked sentences in quick succession. It was obvious, even to Smiffy, he was not thinking the same way as he was talking.

"Let me have another look at him...just to check he's OK, of course." Steinn parted the tarpaulin curtains.

Albert was concentrating hard on his telepathy and was not at first aware of his visitor. Suddenly he had a deep feeling of foreboding, as he picked up Steinn's thoughts and read his intentions.

'Just the right height and weight to act as a donor body for the brain.' Steinn was thinking. 'If it's a success he'll believe he is Uncle Enrico. If it's a failure he'll be in the caustic tank and gone. Either way there'll be no evidence to pin it on me. I will appear absolutely blameless.'

Albert gulped at the cold blooded plan. Now it was even more imperative he made his escape. He sat in silence until Dr Steinn left him in peace, then he hurriedly checked the cage again, hoping against hope for some way of escape he may have missed. He stood in the centre of the floor and inspected the entire prison.

The iron bars were too thick to bend. The sheer brick walls ran right up to the flat roof of the building, where a translucent skylight let in a glimmer of daylight. There was no way he could climb the thirty feet high walls or the bars. The door was securely locked from the outside. That cage had been constructed to hold a large dangerous animal. For a brief moment he wondered just what sort of animal this place was designed to imprison. Was it for lions or tigers, even large dogs? It was then it dawned on him for the first time, the Gryphon may be just such a creature and the mythical beast could well have originated in this building, instead of being conjured up by his ceremonies. Feverishly he pursued the idea. What if they had made the Gryphon? If they had the technology to join one man's body to another man's brain, making a Gryphon by surgically joining together a bird and an animal would not be beyond their capabilities. He knew there were drugs available that prevented tissue rejection. He'd heard of people taking them after a kidney transplant in hospital. Maybe Dr Steinn even had the technology to clone such a creature? Albert wasn't sure what cloning meant, but he'd read about it in the newspapers and he knew science had gone a long way with the concept.

Albert shook his head in dismay. He had misread the situation and landed himself in a very dangerous situation. By searching for the Gryphon, he had put his own life in jeopardy. It was no use telling his captors he had made a mistake about the Gryphon. Things had moved on too far since they first captured him. Now this Dr Steinn had earmarked his body to house some very important brain. "God knows why, at my age!" Albert cried.

Finally, unable to see any other way out, Albert decided he must concentrate on the levitation exercises. They were his only hope. At least, if he perfected that skill, there was a chance he could rise above them and keep out of their reach. He sat in the centre of the cage, took up the lotus position and started feverishly studying levitation anew.

Chapter Thirty

At 6 o'clock in the evening, Armstrong and Smiffy went home from work. Building 37 became very quiet. Apart from the occasional snuffle from a dog and the patter of rats' feet, as they ran up and down the exercise ladders in their cages, Albert was left in peace. He stood up from the lotus position and stretched his legs. Concentrating for so long, and sitting unmoving in one position for hours on end, didn't do his old joints any favours. He walked up and down his prison cell to get his legs back in working order.

At 7 o'clock, Dr Steinn unlocked the door to the building and went through the security doors to his private laboratory. His first concern was to check on the professor's brain, which he found was failing fast.

"Hang on in there, Uncle. I will put you back in your body before the night is out. Then we can discuss your latest research. I'll start once it gets dark and all the day staff have gone." Dr Steinn talked to the glass tank containing the brain, hoping the old man could still hear him. Next he decided to check on his

247

prisoner, before he prepared the operating room for the imminent transplant.

Albert heard the security door open and close and listened to the doctor's footsteps as they stalked down the room towards him. He sat down and resumed the lotus position with his back to the bars, trying to ignore his visitor.

"How are you?" Steinn asked, his voice oozing simulated care. "Don't worry. It will all be over by tonight."

Albert shuddered inwardly as he detected the real thoughts behind the pretence.

I shall have to use a stun dart through the bars, to put the old chap out. Steinn thought.

Albert got the unspoken message. That meant he could still be vulnerable if he was hovering above head height. He had to think again about his plans. And fast! He sat very still, knowing he couldn't make a move with Steinn still watching over him. He decided on one last burst of mental energy to call for help while he had time.

In the woods outside the perimeter fence, two of the druids crept up to the barbed wire in the failing light, to reconnoitre the area.

"There's something hanging on that razor wire." The taller druid pointed to the scrap of Albert's belt, blowing in the breeze.

"It looks awfully like a piece of white towelling belt. I bet that's where Pollawsdoc went over the wire." The other druid whispered.

"But how did he ever climb over that high barbed wire?"

"Search me! But we use wire cutters first."

"Look over there. Security cameras! Don't move fast we may be spotted!"

They crept away into the woods, out of sight of any curious security guards.

Jim, the young plumber's mate, was sitting in his tent with a few friends, sipping mugs of tea and waiting for the elders to give them their orders. Suddenly he clutched his head and groaned.

"Eh up! What's t' matter, Jim?" His mate had noticed the sudden movement.

"I felt queer, just then. I had this vision of this old man in a white dressing gown. He's in a cage in that building over there." Jim pointed to the roof of building 37, which was just visible over the treetops.

"First you feel it in your water, now you're having visions. I don't like this at all!"

One of the other lads, with a modicum of common sense, broke into the conversation. "The chief druid said we were to keep a listening brief for any mental messages that Pollawsdoc sent out. You'd better tell him what you saw."

Jim looked startled. "It's nothing, honestly. 'Appen it was only a headache and my imagination. I've never had any of this 'ere telepathy before."

"Says you. How would you know what it was if you've never had it before? There's got to be the first time for everyone. Come on. I'll take you t' chief druid."

The whole group lifted Jim bodily from the floor and took him to Entwhistle's tent.

"Tell me again lad, what t' vision said." The old druid was excited at this breakthrough, because not one of his expert group had had any luck with ESP. However, he needed to be sure in his own mind that it was a genuine message and not some fabrication of the lad's over active imagination.

"I saw this old fellow in a white dressing gown, sitting in a cage. He told me he was in building 37."

"Building 37?" The druid was at a loss to understand this reference.

"Aye. 'e said it was that one over there." Jim pointed towards the roof of the animal house.

"That fits! That building is near where we saw the white belt on the barbed wire." A taller druid exclaimed.

Entwhistle still wasn't satisfied. "What was he doing, this old man? Was he sitting at a table, or what?"

"No he was in a prison cell with straw on the floor. He was sitting in the lotus position."

"That settles it!" Druid Entwhistle smiled a relieved smile. "Well done lad. When this business is over, you and I must have a chat about advanced mental training for you." He patted Jim on the shoulder.

Jim's mate shook his head. Jim had seemed such a normal sort of chap. 'Appen there's nowt so queer as folk. All t' world's queer but Jim and me, and 'appen even he's a little queer, now,' he thought philosophically.

With their goal now known, the older druids held a council of war to decide exactly how they would free Pollawsdoc, once it got dark.

As the evening light faded, scores of young men began to assemble on the roadway leading to the main gate of the Steinn plant. Dickinson, true to his word, had contacted every one of his animal rights buddies and had organised a large demonstration. They held up their banners and advanced on the main gates.

Tony, with Diana and Reynard in his car, arrived on the scene just as Dickinson and his cohorts moved forward.

"Good timing!" Rey Muldoon shouted. Turning to Diana, he checked his pistol, pushed it into the blouse of his tracksuit, and jumped out of the car. "I will cut the wire when I'm close to building 37. Wish me luck." With a patter of running shoes he vanished into the woods.

Reynard ran alongside the perimeter fence until he came to the part where the white towelling still fluttered in the breeze. He did not go deeper into the woods, so he was totally unaware of the hundred or so druids camped there, and his presence was equally unknown to them The security guards were not so ill informed.

As soon as he started to run along the fence the cameras picked up his quick movements and relayed a picture back to the main office. The Chief of Security enlarged the picture on his screen and gave out his orders.

"That's not one of those demonstrators. Most of those are only kids. This one looks older and fitter. Send a dozen men to the fence where the old chap came over. I think we have his accomplice here." His lieutenant rushed out, to go and organise it.

"Make sure my men are armed." The chief shouted after his man. "I've a gut feeling about this one. I've been expecting something of this sort since we captured that other spy."

Reynard sprinted along the fence in the failing light, clutching his gun to his chest, completely oblivious to the fact that his every move was being closely observed.

At the main gate, Tony and Diana joined the protestors to make as much noise and disturbance as possible. Dickinson, with a little encouragement from his teacher, picked up some stones from the roadside and started to throw them at the security guard's hut. They bounced on the roof and clattered onto the tarmac driveway. The man inside panicked and called for urgent reinforcements.

A dozen tough looking security men ran to the main gate, to keep out the intruders. Dickinson was elated at the chaos they were causing. He grinned at

Tony and shouted. "Good on yer, Sir! Those little animals will thank you for this."

Tony smiled wanly back at the lad. He only hoped they wouldn't all finish up in gaol!

Diana stayed well back from the front line and watched anxiously for signs that Muldoon had managed to get into the plant undetected.

Muldoon crouched by the fence, took the wire cutters from his pocket and clipped his way through the perimeter defence. He kept a sharp lookout, but he had no way of seeing the welcoming party waiting for him behind building 37. He crept through the hole in the wire and ran straight into the arms of the security guards. They jumped on him en mass. He didn't stand a chance. He may have been a trained soldier but one man against twelve burly armed guards was too much of a bad thing. He pulled his gun out, but they were too quick for him. His wrists were snatched and twisted behind his back. Reynard Muldoon managed to fire one single warning shot into the ground before he went under.

The sound of a single gunshot reverberated among the trees. In the chief druid's tent the council of war came to an abrupt halt. The Clogarte experts exchanged knowing glances. They now knew they could be up against armed men.

At the main gate, Diana heard the gunshot with a sinking heart. She recognised it as a pistol shot, and she knew Muldoon would only fire his gun if he was under attack. With only one gunshot fired, the chances were he was captured, or at best pinned down by superior forces. Things were not going to plan.

At the front gate it was stalemate. Tony and the protestors continued their stoning of the security post. The guards decided to wait for an issue of shields and batons before they made a move. The balance of power was very evenly matched. Suddenly several cars drew up on the road behind the protestors, reinforcements had arrived. Tony and Diana looked anxiously at the new vehicles. Were they trapped between the gates and newly arrived security guards?

"Yoohoo! Tony!" A familiar female voice broke the tension.

"Mum! What the devil are you doing here?"

Twenty or so middle aged and elderly ladies, dressed in tracksuits, rushed from the vehicles.

"Now then, tell me what's going on, Tony." Freda rolled up her sleeves for business.

Diana butted into the conversation. "Don't get involved Mrs Tompkins, leave it to the young ones."

Freda scowled at the girl, silencing her with one withering look. Turning to her son she asked. "Is that where your Uncle Albert is being held?"

"We think so, Mum, but..." He got no further. Freda flanked by her WI friends stalked up to the main gate of the plant and beckoned the security guards to come and talk to her. Thinking he was facing a helpless old lady, the leader stepped forward, lowering his baton.

"Step out of my way, young fellow. We're coming in to rescue my brother." Freda informed him flatly.

"No madam, I don't think…" He got no further. Freda threw him to the ground and put an armlock on him. Pandemonium broke out immediately.

"Good on yer, missus!" Dickinson yelled at the top of his voice. He had not enjoyed himself so much since Cup Final Day.

One of the guards rang the security chief. "Help! We are under attack from Hell's Grannies!" he yelled down the phone.

The other members of the WI self-defence class tackled the remaining guards who retreated rather than face such fury. They ran for the shelter of the nearest building, regrouped and took out their tear gas guns.

"Fire in the air, men." The order was given. The canisters of gas arced towards the gate scattering the protestors and WI alike. Thick acrid smoke billowed across the roadway. Figures coughed and spluttered in the fumes, unable to see or take deep breaths. Tony and Diana, clutching handkerchiefs to their faces, rushed in to rescue what members of the WI they could see, and dragged them away from the fighting.

The security chief, sitting safely in his operations office, decided to send six of the men who had captured Muldoon, to reinforce the main gate. He also rang the Runford police and the fire service, telling them the plant was under attack from protestors and possibly on fire.

The druids, unaware of the chaos at the gates, bowed their heads in unison, uttered a resounding 'Ohm' and girded themselves for battle. It was going to be a night to remember.

Chapter Thirty One

Inside building 37, Steinn put the finishing touches to his preparations to transplant the brain into the prisoner's body.

Albert concentrated as he had never concentrated before. The sounds of fighting at the main gates had not penetrated through to either of them.

The security chief had informed Steinn when they had captured Muldoon. He telephoned his boss to let him know everything was under control.

Dr Steinn was livid at being interrupted in his preparations. He had so little time to perform the sensitive operation, without being interrupted constantly.

"That's fine. Now, no more interruptions! If it happens again, whatever the reason, you are fired! What the hell do you think I pay you for? You don't need to tell me every time you do something right! What do you want, a medal?" He slammed the receiver down in a temper, breaking the telephone off the wall bracket and effectively cutting himself off from the outside world.

Albert sat in the lotus position and concentrated on weightlessness. Gradually he felt himself go light. Slowly he felt the floor drop away from his buttocks as he rose gently into the air. He recited the weight reducing mantra even more rapidly, cutting out everything around him. He was so focused he did not hear Frank Steinn come through the security door into the main animal hall.

Dr Steinn stopped at Armstrong's desk and loaded the stun gun with anaesthetic. He took a few deep breaths to calm himself down from the recent disturbing phone call, and walked unhurriedly towards Albert's cage.

Outside in the woods, the four Clogarte Black Belt experts opened up their small suitcases and slipped their wooden clogs onto their feet. Those traditional Lancashire clogs were ideal for rough terrain, being used for centuries on the cobbled streets of the old cotton towns. The four warriors stood shoulder to shoulder, like martial arts experts in an arcade game, and advanced side by side on the wire perimeter fence. Several yards behind them, the younger druids gathered in awe to watch the advance.

"Go for the gap in t' wire, lads. It'll save time" Entwhistle commanded, as he noticed the hole Muldoon had left behind him.

A warning shot rang out from one of the armed guards still on duty, guarding building 37. The guard stepped out of the shadow of the building and fired another single rifle shot above the druids' heads.

The crowd of young druids hesitated then ran for the cover of the trees.

The four Clogarte Black Belts stood their ground.

The rest of the armed security men moved out of the shadows and held their rifles at the ready. They had never before seen anything like this white clad group; well, not since they had captured Albert.

"It's another group of spies like that old fellow we have inside." One of the guards whispered to his mate. "Do you think they will leap over the fence?"

"Keep back from the fence or we'll shoot to kill." The security guard in charge yelled at the druids.

The four druids stood their ground, staring implacably at their adversaries.

Heartened by the fact they had stopped advancing, the guards moved nearer the wire, standing in a line, shoulder to shoulder, mirroring the formation of the black belted druids.

"Now!" One of the druids shouted aloud.

The guards, startled by this sudden command, fired wildly into the trees.

The four druids dropped to the floor as one man. To the guards, it looked as if they had dived for cover. The Clogarte experts rolled forward flinging their legs in the air at lightning speed. Eight wooden clogs arced into the night sky like avenging angels, speeding towards the unsuspecting security men.

The guards had never seen anything like this before. They had worked out these strange white figures could be martial arts experts of some sort, but they felt completely safe protected by the wire fence.

The wooden missiles fell from the sky, landed unerringly on target. NATO Smart-bombs and radar could not have bettered their collective aim.

"Ee ba gum! Its t' sacrifice throw! An' I've never seen it performed better!" One of the younger druids exclaimed in admiration as a flying clog hit each guard squarely on the side of his head, felling him to the ground and knocking the rifle from his hands.

With a roar, ferocious enough to frighten a pride of lions, the four warriors jumped through the gap in the fence and attacked the disorganised guards.

The younger druids attempted to follow their leaders, but enthusiasm got the better of them and they jammed themselves in the narrow gap, a jumble of flailing arms and legs, unable to move.

The security guards had dropped their guns, but thanks to their protective headgear, they recovered from the surprise attack, regrouped quickly and drew their batons. They were determined to stop the intruders getting to building 37 at any price.

The Clogarte experts grinned with pleasure. They had used their secret weapon to good effect. Now, with the loss of the guns and the fight more evenly matched they would enjoy practising their other martial arts. They attacked the six men with every throw and hold in the Clogarte repertoire.

Inside building 37, Dr Steinn pulled back the tarpaulin covering to Albert's cage and sighted along the barrel of his stun gun. To his surprise there was no one in the cage to aim at.

"Impossible!" He roared. "The door is still locked. There's no way he can get out!"

Albert, from his position near the ceiling, heard the roar of rage. He kept his cool and pushed harder on the skylight in the roof. He had succeeded in levitating to the very top of his prison and he had no intention of falling into Steinn's hands. The roof light gave way with a resounding crack. The man below could not help but hear it.

"What the hell! How has he managed to scale those walls?" Steinn rushed to Armstrong's desk to get the key to the cage. If he could open the door, he could still shoot the stun dart into the prisoner's body, from below.

Albert grabbed the edge of the roof and hauled himself out into the moonlight.

"Damn and blast the man!" From below Albert heard the voice of a very frustrated Dr Steinn, but he paid no heed to it. He calculated it would take some time for the doctor to get out of the building and climb up onto the roof. Before that happened, Albert was determined to set free one more prisoner. He ran over the roof to look down on the Gryphon's cage.

Steinn was not so easily thwarted. He rushed over to the mobile gantry he had erected beside the cryogenic tank and pushed it towards an area of floor beneath another of the roof lights. Temper gave him strength. He man-handled the heavy structure into position at a surprising speed.

Albert leaned from the roof and pulled a hole in the net covering the Gryphon's cage. Below him he could hear the animal screeching and running about.

"Come on my beauty." Albert coaxed the hybrid. "Come to Albert. I wont harm you." With a little help from Albert it struggled through the hole in the netting and stood free on the rooftop.

The Gryphon spread its wings and flew up towards the friendly voice.

Albert wrapped his arms around its neck and talked soothingly to it, but he was wasting precious time. He was totally unaware that Steinn had almost forced another of the roof lights open.

At the main gate, the fire brigade had turned the hoses on the smoke bombs and had quickly cleared the air. The police rounded up most of the demonstrators and were talking to the security guards, trying to ascertain what was going on. Tony and Diana slipped away unnoticed into the chemical plant and made their way towards the noise of the fighting they could hear near building 37.

The Clogarte Black Belts were really enjoying themselves, taking revenge on the men who had shot at them. They threw them everywhere in turn, until every guard was either unconscious or had surrendered. This was precisely the instant Tony and Diana arrived on the scene. The martial artists turned to face them, thinking they were reinforcements for the guards.

Tony took in the threat at a glance and realised these druids looked just like his Uncle Albert.

"I'm here to rescue Pollawsdoc. He's my uncle."

They heard his shout and their threat turned into a greeting.

Above all this fighting, Albert was stroking the Gryphon and trying to calm it down, when Steinn pushed open the skylight and scrambled onto the rooftop.

Too late Albert realised he had been caught on the roof with no easy way of escaping.

Below building 37, Diana was searching for Muldoon. As his superior officer she was worried for his welfare. In the shadow of the building's double doors, she found him lying on the ground, his hands and feet secured with plastic ties, his mouth taped over and a blindfold covering his eyes. Diana looked scathingly at her assistant. She bent down and ripped off the tape, before she cut the ties and pulled off the blindfold. Tony winced at the violence of her actions. What a way to have a close shave!

"Get up Muldoon. You made a right mess of that mission." Diana showed him no sympathy.

Muldoon stood rigidly to attention and looked sheepishly down at her feet. "Sorry ma'am. I was outnumbered."

"That's the last chance you get. It's back to the Marines and square bashing for you. Now get this door undone, we need to find Albert Williams before it's to late"

"Stand back, miss. 'appen we can help." One of the larger members of the Clogarte brigade put on his fighting clogs and took a running jump at the metal doors. He hit the obstacle squarely, with both feet, forcing one of the doors completely off its hinges. With a resounding crack the door caved in and light flooded from within, illuminating the yard. The group peered into the building, temporarily blinded by the brightness of the lights.

Dickinson, who had managed to get away from the police in the confusion at the gate, rushed past them into the animal house.

"You are all going to be free!" He shouted. "You'll never forget this glorious night." He ran up and down the cages, opening every door and letting out the experimental animals caged inside. In a matter of minutes the whole floor was one mass of hopping rabbits, scurrying rats and mice, and barking dogs.

On the rooftop, hidden from the searchers below them, Frank Steinn sneered at the figure in the white dressing gown, dropped onto one knee, and took careful aim with his stun gun. But he had reckoned without the Gryphon.

The Eagle-dog screeched in fury and launched itself towards the gunman.

Steinn pulled the trigger just as the hybrid leapt at him. The dart bounced uselessly off the feathers of one of the creature's wings.

The Gryphon landed on Steinn before he was aware of his danger. It clawed at him with its hooked talons, attaching itself firmly to his green operating gown. The hybrid's powerful beak tore at his face, driving the doctor across the rooftop.

Albert watched in horror as the struggling figures reached the end of the flat roof and teetered on the very edge. They fought furiously for some seconds. The Eagle/dog clawed and tore at its creator. Steinn screamed in pain and struggled to get away from the avenging creature. As if in slow motion, the man and the hybrid hesitated at the very edge of the roof. Steinn stepped back with one foot onto the spouting, which gave way under his weight. The adversaries overbalanced and fell into the darkness.

For a second or two Albert was rooted to the spot in horror, then he shook off his fears and rushed to the place where they had vanished. As he ran, he heard the man scream as he fell, then there was an almighty splash as they hit the surface of the caustic solution.

Albert stopped at the very edge of the roof and stared down through the shadows at the ripples on the surface of the caustic soda solution. In the moonlight he could see nothing had floated up to the top. He realised from the greasy appearance of the solution in the tank, that it was some kind of chemical storage, but he hadn't a clue what it was or why Steinn had used it.

"That's the end of my Gryphon. What a way to go." Albert wiped a tear from his eye at this destruction of his dreams. As he stared over the spouting at the moon's reflection, riding over the gurgling surface below him, he became aware of urgent voices calling him from below.

"Is that you, Uncle Albert?" He heard the unmistakable sound of his nephew, Tony, amongst the murmur of male voices.

"Yes. It's me boy. Can you get me down?"

"I think there's a fire escape the other side of that roof." Tony remembered Dickinson's escapade on the school visit. He ran around the building to help his uncle climb safely down the steps.

"Are you alright, Uncle. What's going on? What are you doing up here?" Tony joined the old man on the edge of the roof and peered down at the caustic solution.

"Nothing, Tony. Just wishing things could have been different." There was a sob in the old man's voice as the words caught in his throat.

Tony wasn't sure what Albert meant but his main concern was for his Uncle's safety.

"I think we've had enough excitement for one night. Lets get you home."

Albert shrugged his shoulders and turned to lean on his nephew. He was suddenly feeling his age. As the old man turned to leave the roof, he heard a distant screech from the direction of his woods.

"Did you hear that?" Albert stopped in his tracks and gripped his nephew's hand.

"Yes, I heard it. Was it an owl?"

Albert closed his eyes and concentrated hard on contacting the Gryphon. Above their heads in the darkness, they heard the faint sound of wing beats, then another loud screech. A large shadow passed between them and the moon.

"That was close! My God, it looked big! What was it?" Tony exclaimed.

Albert didn't reply, but he threw his arms around his nephew and hugged him. He had a good idea what it was. Throwing off his feelings of old age, he skipped across the flat roof to the fire escape, for he was certain the Gryphon had lived to fly another day.

Chapter Thirty Two

At 9 o'clock next morning, being Saturday, the bar at the Duck and Dumplings was almost deserted. Paddy was pulling a first pint for Tony Tompkins when the door swung open and Uncle Albert walked in. The barman could not resist a sly glance at the old man's attire. He was relieved to see Albert was dressed perfectly normally.

"Ah! I thought I might find you in here, Tony boy." Albert sat down on a stool next to his nephew. "I'll get that for you. I owe you one." He pulled out his wallet and paid for both of their drinks.

"Are you OK? Did you sleep well?" Tony enquired.

"Fine. Slept like a baby, in my own bed."

The bar man, who always kept an ear open for any gossip, asked. "Have either of you heard anything about the Steinn plant?"

They both looked at him and shook their heads.

"Oh! Only I heard they had a spot of bother there last night. Some rockers at a music festival, fighting with animal rights protestors."

"I don't know what the world's coming to." Albert grunted. "I hope they stayed out of my woods."

Tony got off his stool and ushered his Uncle to a table in the far corner, where they could talk privately.

"Well? What's happening now?"

"Nothing."

"Nothing? What about this Archdruid business?"

"I'm not interested. There's nothing in it for me. Besides what do I want with hundreds of dedicated followers at my time of life? If I was that desperate for company I'd get married...and I've no intention of doing that." The old man smiled enigmatically.

"But what about the lessons you paid for, and your training? What about Pollawsdoc?"

"Pollawsdoc no longer exists. I had a package from that imposter Modnoc waiting for me at home. He returned my photograph and my money. Talk of a solicitor must have frightened him."

"What about the Wise One and his lot?

"I've had a word with Entwhistle, the chief druid...he's a nice bloke you know, used to be a Nat West manager...Anyway, I explained the excitement was no good for me, at my age."

Tony frowned. Had the last few days really upset the old chap's health? Then he noticed the twinkle in his uncle's eyes.

"They took it well, really. It seems they'd really prefer to train a young new Archdruid who can lead them for years to come. They've found a young bloke called Jim something or other; he's a plumber's mate with latent psychic powers." Albert sipped his beer and wiped the froth from his upper lip. "I've donated the tapes and hand written lessons that the Wise One gave me. Jim's a nice lad. I think he'll do well. He's got his feet firmly on the ground."

"No levitation, then?" Tony couldn't resist the pun.

"No, no more levitation for him or for me. In fact I've decided to concentrate on building up the wildlife in my woods. That strikes me as safer than all these religions."

The bar door swung open and Diana Scullery marched briskly in.

"I thought I'd find you here." She walked over to them. "I missed you at the house."

"Sit down young lady." Albert moved his chair to make room for her.

"No thanks. I'm in a hurry." Turning to Tony she took a roll of bank notes from her pocket and handed them to him. "That's my rent to the end of the month. But I will be leaving tonight. Thanks for your help the other night."

"Going so soon? What about school?"

"They have been contacted by my HQ. They'll have to replace Muldoon and myself with supply teachers."

"Where are you going…am I allowed to ask or is it an official secret?"

"I shouldn't really discuss it, but I've had a report that some idiot in Scotland has crossed a python with a turtle and has set it loose in Loch Ness."

Tony exchanged looks with Albert. They both fought valiantly to keep straight faces.

"Will..." Tony's voice rose as he tried to control his mirth. "Will Muldoon be accompanying you?"

"Him! Not likely. I can't use weak men in my job." With that cutting comment, she turned briskly on the spot and marched out of Tony's life.

"Women!" Tony grumbled. "I thought I was on a winner with that one, but instead of a soft feminine girl, she turned out to be a hard, scheming, secret agent and she packed a gun! If you are giving up religion, I'm giving up women!"

"That's a pity then. I'm off home ,to the old country for a two week holiday. We have a gorgeous blonde barmaid standing in for me. She's a bit like yon madam to look at..." The barman nodded his head towards the street door through which agent Scullery had so recently departed. "...but she's bigger up top." He held his hands well out in front of his chest to emphasise the point.

Tony frowned and shook his head, but his eyes were smiling.

"I'll certainly see you in here every night for the next two weeks then?" Albert winked at his nephew, then they both burst out laughing.

The End